SOULS
INTERTWINED

NENAYA RENEE

Souls Intertwined

First Printing: 2015

Published in the United States of America

So Addictive Mindz Publications

ISBN 978-1-505-37054-6

www.nenayarenee.com

| DEDICATION

I dedicate this book to everyone that has ever motivated me, supported me, prayed for me, and believed in me as I sought out to accomplish a goal I didn't think I would ever achieve.

| ACKNOWLEDGMENTS

Humbled thanks to the man that has kept me on this earth for the past twenty eight years of my existence so that I am able to do what I love and share it with the world. He keeps blessing me even when I may not deserve it and that requires the biggest thank you.

To my family and friends, I love you all. Hearing "I am so proud of you" has been the biggest motivation throughout this process. I can't thank you enough for your continued support, it means everything to me.

To everyone that has taken the time to buy this book supporting my dream, you are dope! Thank you so very much.

| PROLOGUE

I tuck the very last photo behind the protective cover, smooth it with a firm hand, and sit back to admire my work. I have been functioning on this book for weeks, a gift for my wife. For years, she has kept precious memories stored away in a worn cardboard box that sat in the top of the downstairs coat closet up until today. She keeps saying she will get around to sorting through it but something more appealing always seems to draw her away from the task. I shut the book close, finger the gold cover that has a picture of us on our wedding day in the designated frame. To think, it has been five years since we got married. Time is hasty but I have enjoyed every passing minute of it.

"Daddy, daddy...can I go with Jaime to the park?"

She is her mother with those slanted grey eyes, impeccable golden brown skin, and long curly hair that falls down her back. Somehow she managed to inherit my nose and dimpled smile but there is no denying that Farah spit her out. Quickly, I hide the book with a manila folder overflowing with paperwork for a twelve month project I have been working on.

"You know I don't like you two going places alone."

I am overprotective of my child and well within right. The world just isn't what it used to be when I was growing up. My mother used to push my brother and I out of the door every day after our homework was finished to go somewhere and play until it got dark. She never worried and she never had to. Now, with all the fanatical shit happening around us, I second guess letting her out of my sight with fear that something may happen to her. She bats her long eyelashes at me, folds her lips into a pout. No matter how many times she does this to me and I say I won't fall for it again, I always manage to fall victim to it anyway. She is without doubt a daddy's girl.

"How about I take you two instead?"

Her eyes light up as she hauls herself into my lap, latching her arms around my neck in a hug.

"Thank you!"

"Yeah, yeah...you and Jaime go put your sneakers and jacket on. Tell your mother to come on too."

She makes a beeline for the door, yells over her shoulder. "Ok daddy."

Certain that the coast is clear, I retrieve the photo album from its hiding spot, quickly shoving it inside of the bottom desk drawer.

"Grayson, I really don't want to go to the park."

She stands in the doorway, her hands planted firmly on her hips staring at me through forceful grey eyes. She is by far the most beautiful woman I have ever laid eyes on. I feel accomplished when I see men cock their heads to stare at her in public. I got that, she belongs to me. I do a quick once over to make sure there are no traces of my secret project visible before standing to my feet. I invade her space with my 6'3 stature; bend to kiss her lips that are turned up into a frown.

"For me, please."

"Grayson, I'm really tired," she whines.

I press my lips to the corners of her mouth, trails kisses across her cheek before settling them against the base of her neck.

"I know you are but you need to walk that baby out or let me..."

She shoves me playfully. "You're so nasty."

"And you love it."

She stares up at me, a rousing passion has replaced the displeased look she was giving me just minutes before.

"Lucky for you, I do." She sighs heavily. "Fine, I will go. Let me grab my sneakers."

I smile at my successful persuasion.

"Thank you."

She cuts her eyes at me.

"Grayson Powell, you owe me."

I reach out cradling her protruding belly in my overbearing hands, palm it like Spalding. In a few more weeks, we will be the parents of a baby boy; a mini me, my junior.

"Daddy will make it up to you," I tell her with a seducing tone.

"Give me a kiss, daddy."

My lips are back on hers, her hands cupping my face as her tongue invites me in. My erection throbs. Now I wish I would have just said yes to the children going to the park alone. I am ready to take my wife to bed and lose myself in the softest place on earth.

"There won't be any parks to go to if you don't go put those sneakers on."

She draws my bottom lip in through her teeth tugging gently. Her hand finds its way to the seat of my pants, cradling my hard-on in her palm. "Lets pick this up later."

Fighting the urge to pull her inside of my office and make love to her on my desk, I watch her turn and walk away. She possesses enough confidence to capture a room; she can put any woman to shame. She is everything...my entirety, my world. Farah Powell is an amazing woman and I knew that from the very day I met her...

"When I met you, everything seemed perfect..."

- Farah Acosta

I Mr. Brown Skin

Fuck love; plain and simple. Everyone around me is married or engaged and the whole while, I'm just trying to make it home on time to see *Scandal* every Thursday. My love life is pretty damn pathetic and it has been for some time now. The last real relationship I had was with Calvin Ethers, a tall, dark skin specimen with a great personality and amazing sex. I loved him. I would have bet my last dollar that he and I were going to be together for the rest of our lives. I would have been broke as fuck too!

"I'm not ready for this."

He had buttered my ass up real good before we left my apartment. Sexed me up something proper in the shower, had a sister damn near comatose afterwards. You can only imagine my surprise when he uttered those five words to me.

"I really like you Farah but this shit is just going way too fast. I think we need to slow down a bit, take a break."

Like me? Take a break? Just an hour ago, he was groaning in my ear how much he loved me and now he was hollering about taking a break. I was two seconds from setting it off in that restaurant; ready to act my entire color. His black ass should have been running up out of there with my size seven dangling from the crack of his ass. I glared at him through ballistic grey eyes from across the dinner table. Till this day, he should be thanking the homie upstairs that I didn't slap earth, wind, and fire out of his trifling behind. Yup, I kept it cool. I didn't want to give him the satisfaction of being the angry black woman. Instead, I launched my balled up napkin at him and walked out. Of course I didn't drive! That would have just made *too* much sense, right. So there I was looking like a damn fool walking the streets of DC while I hollered into the receiver of my cell phone for my sister to pick me up. His bitch ass had the audacity to text me, *text* me, later on that night to say that he never meant to hurt me and he wished me well in my future. I was so over it, I was under it. I responded back that his shit would be sitting on the curb outside of my apartment building waiting for pick-up or the garbage man, whoever got to it first. Needless to say, I never heard from him after that episode. Once the anger subsided, the blow of having lost the man I loved hit me hard. I coped as best I could until it became easier to deal with. I became numb and eventually I disconnecting myself from it altogether. That was two years ago. And now, here I am a twenty-eight year old single woman and not exactly sure *how* to mingle.

"Can I get you something to drink while you wait?"

She can't be much older than eighteen, twenty max with dirty blonde hair and piercing blue eyes. She introduces herself as Sarah.

"A glass of your house red wine please," I tell her without looking at the menu.

She smiles sweetly before walking off.

I am sitting at a table tucked away in a corner of *Clyde's*, a quaint American restaurant off of M street in DC, the picturesque window giving view to the evening traffic and crowded streets. Feeling awkward for sitting alone, I busy myself with the menu waiting impatiently for my best friend and sister to arrive. The waitress is back faster than she had left placing a long stem wine glass in front of me. With a forced smile, I tell her thank you.

"Sorry...no, excuse me."

I look up to see my sister, Clarissa Davis, doing the church scoot through the narrow aisle in an attempt to get to the table.

"Damn! You would think with all the business this place gets, they would expand this bitch. I had my ass all on somebody's shoulder, shit is out of hand."

She plops down into one of the empty chairs.

"Traffic is a monster and parking ain't any better."

The last days of fall are turning cold indicating that the winter months are upon us. Clarissa eases out of her leather coat hanging it on the back of her chair, loosens her scarf letting it dangle around her neck. She is a shade darker than me with light brown almond shaped eyes and dark brown hair she keeps cut short just below her ears. Towering over me by two inches, she is rather petite in frame with small hips and a big behind.

"Long day?" she quizzes, eyes me as I sip from my glass.

"Nope, I just like to drink," I mutter sarcastically.

She rolls her eyes at me flipping open the menu.

"Smart ass, where is Terri?"

"She should be on her way."

I pull my cell phone from my purse to check the time. It is a Friday evening, almost six-thirty though it feels later. Outside, the day has come and gone. The sky is now dark and night has fully settled in.

Right on cue, Terri comes pumping through the front door stopping briefly to be pointed in our direction by the hostess. I have known Terri soon-to-be Andrews since our freshman year at *Norfolk State University*. She was my very first roommate, my *only* roommate to be matter of fact. We have been thick as thieves ever since. Terri has flawless dark brown skin, big brown eyes, and legs for days. She really could have been a model, as beautiful as she is, but her undying passion to teach children overshadowed those ambitions. Born and raised in Jamaica, her family moved to Virginia when she was thirteen. Despite all of her years living here, she has never lost that Jamaican drawl.

"Ladies, how are you?"

Terri flashes her million dollar smile easing into the other empty chair.

She looks nothing short of amazing in her dark pink wrap dress and multi-colored heels. Her long, beautiful dreads are pulled up high atop her head in a neat bun.

"Don't you look good or whatever," Clarissa pipes. "I *love* that color on you!"

"Thanks girl, Raymond bought it for me."

Clarissa reaches out to feel the fabric.

"He has good taste."

Before they can indulge in their conversations of husbands, what they do and don't do, and other shit I prefer not to talk about as a single woman, the waitress emerges to take their drink orders.

"How was everyone's day?" Clarissa asks.

I am sitting at a table of well educated, beautiful women of color. Terri is a college professor, my sister a paralegal, and I a family counselor. We ooze prestige.

"It was another typical Friday, different week," I state unenthused.

Shortly after graduate school, I came back home to Alexandria to intern for a woman named Audrey, whom my mother is great friends with, that owns a family counseling firm. For one year I fetched her coffee, took her messages, organized her schedule, and shadowed her sessions. I was a regular ole pro by the time I made it on the actual payroll. Two years ago, Audrey suffered a stroke and was forced to retire decreasing the office down to four women. Excuse me while I toot my own horn when I say my dedication and hard work paid off when she placed me as the executive manager and head counselor. I have counseled young girls that were once victims of rape, families that have lost a child and even women unable to bear children. One of my main clients, particularly, Ms. Frasier, pulled her daughter into my office after learning she was skipping school to have sex with boys much older than she. Ms. Madeline Frasier, a recent divorcee and a working woman of two jobs, sat sobbing in my office this morning.

"I don't know what else to do," she says. "I can't control her. She's slipping between my fingers."

I fish a few dollar bills out of my purse for her daughter Cynthia Frasier to go ball out at the vending machines down the hall while I speak to her mother in private.

"Is there any family she can stay with for a little while?" I ask handing her a fistful of tissues.

She dabs at her cheeks and nose. "My brother and I have been talking this over for some time now. He lives in Texas and we think maybe she is better off staying with him awhile."

She needs her little ass whooped, I think consoling the crying mom.

I think of all the times my mother broke open a can of whoop ass on me. Shit, I could only wish somebody would ship me off some damn where. Nonetheless, whether Cynthia likes it or not, she will be on her way to Texas in a few months. Ms. Frasier will allow her to finish out the school year before sending her off. Our sessions will continue on as normal until her departure.

"I don't see how you can work with troubled families all day," Clarissa says. "I would have lost my entire damn mind by now, somewhere sobbing and shit."

"That's why people hire you to win cases."

Terri shakes her head in agreement, says, "Girl, I feel you. I think the same thing and I teach adults all damn day. These college kids have no appreciation of the privilege to further their education. They spend all that damn money not to show up for days at a time but want to mysteriously start turning in assignments and shit before the end of the semester. I happily fail all of them. At the end of the day, it's their money not mine."

We laugh.

"Speaking of cases, I have been hired to take on a divorce case and this bad boy is going to get real ugly!"

Clarissa pauses long enough to let the waitress take our food orders and set down the drinks.

"What was I saying? Oh yeah, so they have money...so much money it's ridiculous. They have joint accounts this and properties that. All that shit has to be divided up amongst them. Bad part is majority of the assets come from her business and now she has to trick off half of it to her ex-husband's greedy ass. You ever just look at a man and tell he ain't about shit? That's him. I love my husband and all but I have to have my own. God forbid we ever get a divorce, I am not going through all of that."

Terri waves a testifying hand in the air.

"Amen sister, Amen. And speaking of husbands, I have to push the time of the dress fittings up to noon on Saturday."

Three months shy of the big day, I am overly anxious to witness my best friend get married. I have been there for her through the happiest of times and her shoulder to cry on through the hardest. I know she will make an exceptional wife. Even more, I know her wedding is going to turn out to be amazing.

The waitress arrives with our food: Shrimp and grits for Clarissa, chicken seafood pasta for Terri, and a salmon salad with raspberry vinaigrette dressing for me. I don't even know the man but I am starving like Marvin! I extended my session with Ms. Frasier, forfeiting my lunch hour, to keep her from having a conniption in my damn office.

Terri swallows a mouthful of food with a gulp of water, dabs at the corners of her mouth with a cloth napkin, and says, "You must know this man memorizing your face at that table over there. I mean he has been *staring* you down girl."

When no one answers, she shoots me a glare like "yeah bitch, I'm talking to you."

I shift in my seat to get a better look at the chiseled piece of heaven sitting at the table a few feet away from us. His brown skin is perfect underneath a full, manicured beard; neat hair cut, and long full eyelashes that shield his puppy dog brown eyes. Sure enough, his gaze is fixed on me, unashamed. If looks were cheap, I would ask for my face back. I don't know him, that is for damn sure but I certainly wouldn't mind getting to know him. Another man joins him at the table peeling his eyes away from me.

"No, he doesn't look familiar," I stammer taken by how attractive he is.

"Well honey, I can't tell."

Color begins to fill my cheeks.

"Girl boo!" I say hiding my emerging smile with my wine glass. "He is not checking for me."

But, in fact, he was.

I am too busy digging around in my make-up case for my lip gloss to notice Mr. Brown Skin when he steps to our table.

"Excuse me ladies."

His voice is deep and sultry, a kissing after dark type of voice. *God his smile is amazing!*

He has the best pair of pearly whites I have ever laid eyes on, just straight and...all there.

"Damn, it took you long enough to get over here! I just thought you were going to keep staring and that's it."

That is Terri cutting the shit and going straight for the jugular. He smiles coolly.

"I was debating," he responds, his eyes fixed on me. "I saw you lovely ladies with wedding rings and I assumed you might have one too. After further admiration, I didn't see one so I came to introduce myself."

And I guess this would be the part where I tell him my name or something along the lines of an appropriate introduction. I would...I mean, I am...but cat has my tongue. I am pinned beneath his stare; I don't even think my brain is on right now.

Clarissa clears her throat loudly.

"At least you have good eyes," she jokes. "I'm Clarissa, this is Terri, and the woman that you've been gawking at is my sister Farah."

My eyes run the length of him admiring his six foot three, muscular build. It is evident he isn't missing any days in the gym.

"It is nice to meet you ladies."

He eases over to my side of the table, holds a large, firm hand in my direction to shake.

"It is especially nice to meet you..."

"It's a pleasure to meet you as well..."

I pause; wait for him to tell me his name.

He delivers, replies, "Grayson Powell."

Grayson Powell, now that has a nice ring to it.

"Yeah, well I don't mean to break up this little meeting," Clarissa announces standing up from her chair. "But I have a husband I need to get home to."

"Ditto," Terri replies.

"My brother and I were just leaving too; let me walk you ladies out."

He grabs my hand into his, helping me to steady my weight as I stand to my five inch heel stiletto feet.

"Thank you Mr. Powell."

"Please Farah, call me Grayson."

"Ok Grayson," I say with a nervous smile.

I put my Jane Hancock on the receipt and leave a few bills for the waitress's tip before following everyone else out of the front door. The temperature has dropped. I pull my blazer tighter around my frame crossing my arms over my chest as a means to provide warmth. I thought I was being cute this morning, leaving the house without bringing my real jacket, but now I wish I had it. An older gentleman with a bald head and a neatly trimmed salt and pepper beard is pacing back and forth in front of the restaurant vigorously texting someone on his cell phone. He is taller than Grayson but not by much and it is no secret he keeps himself in shape too.

"I will talk to you later, Farah, "Clarissa says scooping me up into a hug. "It was nice meeting you, Grayson."

He flashes a *Colgate* smile.

"It was nice meeting you as well. Have a good night."

Terri bids her farewells too and she and Clarissa scurry off down the block toward their cars.

"Farah, this is my brother Elliott."

He is still consumed by his phone but stops briefly to shake my hand.

"It's nice to meet you, Farah."

"You too."

"I don't want to keep you, I know it's cold out here. Is it okay if I take your number and give you a call sometimes?"

Yes the hell you can Grayson Powell!

"Yes, that would be fine."

We pull out our cellular devices to exchange numbers. Elliott's phone rings loudly. He answers almost immediately strolling further down the block away from intruding ears. I don't have to heed his conversation to know whoever is on the other end is getting their ass chewed out. His body language makes that crystal clear.

"If you aren't busy tomorrow, I would love to take you out.

Maybe we can meet up and have brunch or something."

Or casual sex, I think to myself with a laugh.

"Look Gray, I'm going to have to take a rain check for tonight. I have some shit I need to handle."

Elliott is annoyed, his tone is bitter. He shoves his cell phone down into the breast of his jacket.

Grayson frowns disappointingly, says, "No problem bro, some other time."

They exchange a brotherly hug.

"We're still on to ball in the morning though right?"

"Yeah, I'll be there the usual time."

"Cool!"

He is gone, jogging off in the opposite direction to his car. I notice the hint of discontentment on Grayson's face and I immediately feel bad even when I don't know his story or him well enough to understand why I feel as bad as I do.

"It's so early. Would you like to join me for a drink?" I ask before I can fully process my words. It is my attempt at breaking the awkward silence.

Though he is unable to hide the frustration on his face, he smiles.

"Absolutely, I would love that."

Girl, what the hell are you doing?

I don't have answer the first. All I know is my feet are moving and I am trying to get my happy ass out of the cold.

We find a seemingly-quiet-to-be-a-Friday-night lounge a few doors down from *Clyde*'s. We take seats at the bar. A football game is playing on the flat screen television while John Legend's *Ordinary People* floats through the speakers.

"Have you been here before?" I ask rubbing my hands hastily over my arms to create enough friction to warm my body.

He shrugs out of his suit jacket and drapes it over my shoulders.

"I haven't but the atmosphere is nice."

A blush rises to the surface of my face as I accept it thankfully wrapping myself in its heat. I inhale the masculine scent left behind from the traces of his cologne that still linger on the collar. There is nothing like a man in a suit especially one that is sexy and smells good. Inside, I am doing the cabbage patch but I smile warmly on the outside and say, "I agree, it is nice."

We order two Hennessy and Red Bulls by way of a young man with a thick Spanish accent slinging drinks behind the bar.

"So Grayson Powell, nice name by the way, what do you do for a living?"

He loosens his necktie, undoes the first two buttons of his dress shirt, undoes the cufflinks, and rolls up his sleeves. I hope I don't look like a dog salivating at the mouth as I watch his every move. The fabric of his dress shirt hugs his muscles delightfully. I cross my thick thighs one over the other in an attempt to suppress my arousal.

"I manage a small team of computer engineers and architects," he answers proudly. "We're a bunch of nerds in suits."

"And that would make you head nerd in charge, right?"

He chuckles. "Yeah, I guess you can say that."

I am smiling harder than a child getting to pick something out at the grocery store after their mother told them they couldn't have shit before getting out of the car.

"You have beautiful dimples."

The base in his voice thumps right through me. I force my thighs tighter together.

"Thank you. How old are you, Mr. Powell?"

"I just turned thirty two months ago," he says. "And you?"

"I'm twenty-eight."

"I would have never guessed it. You look in your early twenties."

Oh the flattery.

"And you Farah, what is your occupation?"

"I am an executive manager and head counselor for a family counseling firm."

He raises a thick eyebrow at me.

"A beautiful career woman, I like that."

I am blushing again. *Damn you Grayson.* I scramble to take the attention off of me.

"I hope everything is okay with your brother. He seemed pretty pissed off back there."

Grayson rolls his eyes, beautiful brown eyes they are.

"Ever since he filed for his divorce, he's been cussing and fussing out his lawyers and his wife. I'll be glad when the shit, excuse my French, is over."

I take a long drink from my cup. *Papi Chulo behind the bar spared no alcohol making these drinks, damn!*

"I'm guessing you and your brother are close."

"He became my guardian after our parents passed away in a car crash. I was fifteen and he was twenty-one."

I recognize a sadness in his eyes, it's as if a grey cloud has rolled in off the street and perched itself over his head.

"I'm really sorry to hear that Grayson. I didn't mean to stir up old memories."

"Farah..."

"Oh, I'm sorry, Farah Acosta."

"Ms. Acosta, you never get over losing your parents but I'm okay with it now. It still hurts but not as much as it used to."

If I could sink below the floorboards I would. For a moment, I feel bad for having brought up the subject all together. He smiles reassuringly and his little grey cloud scampers away. We talk over a few more drinks about the parts of our lives we aren't afraid to share with strangers. I am intrigued by this man. His presence is alluring and what little I *do* know about him makes him that much more captivating. I'm so warm I'm ready to come out of my clothes and I can't pinpoint whether it's because of him or the drinks.

"I could talk to you all night if you let me," Grayson says sincerely. "Unfortunately, it's getting late and a gentleman never keeps a lady out past midnight."

Damn it, where has the time gone? I think glancing over at the clock on the wall. I hadn't even noticed the hour until he said something.

He signals the bartender over to bring our checks. Without so much as a glance at the bill to check the price, Grayson hands him his credit card.

"Thank you so much Grayson."

The waiter brings his card and the receipt back to be signed. He does a quick incoherent scribble across the paper and hands it back. I reach in my purse and pull a ten dollar bill from my wallet for the tip. Grayson shoots me a displeasing look. I ignore him as I push the money into the man's hand.

"Ms. Acosta..."

He stares into my eyes, penetratingly, reprimanding me for going against him.

"Don't do that again," he mutters tucking his wallet in his pocket as he stands to his feet.

Damn he looks edible when he is borderline upset.

I slide back into my suit jacket and hand him his after coming out of them two drinks ago. Without words, I turn on my heels and lead us to the front door and back out into the frigid air. We walk in silence to my car, the calming kind of silence when two people are merely enjoying each other's company.

"I needed this," Grayson replies holding open the door of my *Nissan Sentra* as I climb in behind the wheel. "Thank you for allowing me to accompany you."

"I can't say I didn't enjoy the company, thank you again."

"I hope to be able to do this again with you soon."

My eyes rest on his full lips as he speaks. I don't know this man from the next Joe Smoe walking down the street but I am completely drawn to him. Slowly, he runs his tongue across his lips sending my hormones spiraling into a tizzy.

"I would like that too. I had a really good time."

He waits until I am tucked inside of the car before closing the door behind me. I rev up the engine and turn the heat on full blast before rolling my window down to say goodbye.

"I meant what I said earlier, if you aren't busy tomorrow I would definitely like to take you out again...without you trying to beat me to the tip."

I chortle. "You're such a tough crowd Mr. Powell. I think I will take you up on that offer though."

He leans into the car window. My breath catches in my throat, I'm reeling from his closeness. Anticipating his kiss, I close my eyes against the friction of his touch. He doesn't kiss me, instead he moves to my ear, whispers, "Get home safely."

He presses his lips on the spot underneath my earlobe. My skin sings igniting a shiver that runs from my head down to the tips of my toes.

"You too," I say hardly above a whisper.

I spool my morals back in after damn near throwing them out of the window. He knows what he's doing.

Grayson stands firm in the spot where my car once was as he watches me back it up out of the parking spot and off into the quieting streets of DC.

Fuck love? Did I say that? No. What I really meant to say is, "Hi, my name is Farah. It's nice meeting you again."

1 DATE NIGHT

"Girl if you don't get your hand out of my damn bacon, you had better!"

I duck a swatting hand unscathed with a piece of bacon. Clarissa narrows her brown eyes at me as I shove the rest of it into my mouth. Just as a balled up piece of paper towel sails in my direction, Anita Acosta sashays into the country styled kitchen. Our mother always knows how to enter a room as if she owns the place. Her hair laid for the straight hair gods in a neatly cut bob that hangs just above her shoulders; a beautiful brown skinned woman with dark brown eyes, deep dimples, and enough hips to give some away and still have a lot left over.

"I can always depend on you two to act like children."

She hugs us smelling of perfumed glory, plants her motherly kisses on our cheeks before taking a seat on one of the stools overlooking the breakfast bar.

"That's what sisters do," Clarissa says grinning over at me as if up to no good. "And guess what mami; Farah met a man last night."

This bitch!

Interested eyes shift in my direction, the attention is on me. I roll my eyes at my sister who is now smirking with victory.

"His name is Grayson Powell, "I mutter. "I met him last night at *Clyde*'s when we went to dinner with Terri, had a few drinks afterward, and I am hoping to see him again later."

Clarissa spins around, surprised. "You didn't tell me about drinks."

I grin; stick my tongue out in her direction.

"You didn't ask."

"Well I am happy you met someone," mami says with a warming smile. "What does this young man look like?"

I smirk at the thought of him.

"He's really good looking, *fine* is a better word."

Mami gives me an approving look.

"Well maybe I will actually get to meet this one."

I cut my eyes at her, frown. *The fuck is that suppose to mean?*

Before I say something to get me slapped down into the floor, I leave to go set the eating table.

It is fifteen minutes until noon, the sun is bright and high in the sky as Clarissa and I cruise along the city streets toward *David's Bridal.*

"If this bitch calls me one more time…"

Clarissa glares at the number appearing on her caller ID. It's Terri…for the fourth time.

"I mean, I told her we would be there in fifteen minutes before we left the house. Damn, I can't wait until this wedding is over. She's going to drive us and her nuts. I wasn't *this* bad when I was planning my wedding, was I?"

I'm happy my phone is buried in the bottom of my purse, I don't have time for Terri's nonsense right now.

I hit my right blinker, turn at the corner. I glance over at her from the corner of my eye, laugh. "Girl please, you had your moments and a whole lot of them actually. Eventually I just started smiling and nodding at everything you said just to keep from choking the shit out of you. By the way, I hated your centerpieces. Those thangs were ugly!"

Clarissa's mouth gapes open.

"Fuck you Farah! What kind of sister are you? Why didn't you tell me?"

"I tried but your ass wasn't trying to hear it so I stopped putting my two cents in."

"Oh bitch whatever, just you wait until you have to plan a wedding."

I ease into a parking spot close to the front door. "Well, lets not hold our breath while we wait, eh?"

Inside Terri is cradling her cell phone between her shoulder blade and ear as she holds up an eggshell colored fabric in front of her. She smiles widely when she sees us coming through the door.

"There you two are!" she exclaims in that thick, islander accent. "I know ya'll see me calling you!"

She quickly presses the end button on her phone call, tucks her cell into the back pocket of her jeans.

"Well bitch, we are here. Where is the damn fire?"

She rolls her eyes, says, "So of course everything is right except the flower girl's dress. It will not be ready for another week and I don't know when my brother or sister-in-law will be able to get back to DC before the wedding to do the fitting for her."

My inner self sucks her teeth. *So that's why you were blowing us up?*

I put a hand on her shoulder and squeeze it reassuringly.

"Girl, you had me thinking something serious happened. Look, don't stress yourself out just yet. You have a little less than three months to do the fitting. We will figure something out."

Terri runs an exasperated hand over her locs, forces a smile. "You sound so sure, I hope you're right."

I pull her into a hug. "I'm the maid of honor; I will make sure it gets done."

This time she smiles with relief.

Clarissa, me, and three other bridesmaids take turns trying on our dresses. As her maid of honor, she settles on a satin, one shoulder Vera Wang gown for me to wear. The dress hugs my curves like a latex glove. A bitch won't be eating for a week if I plan on still fitting this bad boy in a couple more months. While the saleswoman packages our dresses in garment bags and rings them up, I check my phone for messages or missed calls. Aside from the four missed calls from Terri's crazy ass, there is one from Grayson. I am almost unable to contain my eagerness as I slip unnoticeably outside to return his call.

He answers on the second ring. For a moment, in my mind, I imagine him being just as excited to hear my voice, as I am to hear his.

"Hello."

"Good afternoon, Mr. Powell," I say shyly like a girl calling her high school crush for the first time.

He replies, "Good afternoon Ms. Acosta, it's good to hear your voice again."

I flush crimson. "I'm sorry I missed your call. I was in a fitting for my best friend's wedding."

"No need to apologize, I'm just happy you called me back. I was hoping I might be able to take you out for dinner tonight."

Take me anywhere you want Grayson Powell.

I clear my throat in an attempt to hide the excitement building up in my voice.

"I think that can be arranged," I reply unworriedly.

I can hear him smiling through the phone, or maybe it is just my imagination since I am cheesing like a kid on picture day.

"I know this really great authentic Mexican restaurant, if you eat Mexican. I mean, we..."

I say quickly, "No, Mexican is fine."

We agree on eight o'clock for dinner. Though slightly hesitant, I give him my address to pick me up around seven thirty.

"I'm really looking forward to seeing you again," he tells me before we hang up.

This feeling, this giddy feeling is like something I have read in novels. I try to give my inner self a pep talk, tell her to hold her britches just in case this Grayson man turns out to be a waste of time. However, I cannot help this smile and even the cold air is not enough to keep me from melting where I stand.

"Are you going to try on your whole damn closet before you choose an outfit?"

Clarissa sits scowling at me from her seat on the edge of my queen size bed. I stand frowning at the outfit I now have on, at least five other outfits are scattered in my bedroom floor. I am completely indecisive. I examine my light brown skin underneath a pair of blue distressed jeans, an oversized beige sweater, and a pair of dark brown knee high boots. I run a manicured hand over my curly brown hair that hangs longingly down my back whenever it's not pinned up. Underneath elongated eyelashes, I shift my grey eyes over to where my sister is sitting. I have been trying on outfits for the last hour.

Fuck it, I tell myself with a frustrated sigh.

It's five minutes after seven and I don't have hair or makeup the first done. Just as I talk myself out of changing my shirt for the umpteenth time, my cell phone rings. It's Grayson.

"Hello Mr. Powell," I answer.

"Good evening beautiful. I just called to let you know that I am in route."

"I guess I will see you in a few then."

"You most definitely will."

I nearly trip as the sole of my boot catches onto a shirt lying in the floor. Hastily, I grab Clarissa's hand and head for the bathroom.

"He's on his way," I say with slight panic in my voice. "I need help with my hair and make-up."

Clarissa giggles at my flustered nature as she digs into my box of make-up retrieving some eye shadow, brushes, and a handful of lipsticks. I sit down on the edge of my bathtub as she goes to work on my face, her fingers moving swiftly. At some point, Clarissa aspired to be a make-up artist for big name celebrities. Needless to say, that pipe dream never made it off the ground. Within five minutes, my eyelids are the color of gold and dark brown. My lips a beautiful nude color I didn't even know I had buried down underneath a pile of nail polishes. Clarissa pushes my curls over my right shoulder holding them in place with a bobby pin.

"Sis, you look beautiful."

She rears back and admires her work of art, pleased.

I stand to look at myself in the mirror. I look like the girl next door, though sexier.

"Thank you."

She hugs me quickly, ushers me out of the bathroom. I gather my purse and jacket; double check to make sure my pocket knife is tucked safely in a place that is easily accessible. I spray my favorite *Dolce and Gabbana* fragrance on my pressure points. My cell phone in hand, it vibrates with a text message from Grayson letting me know he is downstairs waiting.

Nervously, I turn to look at my sister.

"I haven't seen you this nervous since you were about to walk downstairs to meet your date for the prom. What was his name again?"

I laugh relaxing a little.

"Corey...Corey Phillips. I thought he was so fine."

"I know. You wouldn't stop talking about him. I hope you have a great time tonight, okay. Text me your whereabouts throughout the night just in case I have to send the goons out."

I roll my eyes in her direction.

"Heffa, the only goon you know is that fool David that works at *CVS* that's been trying to get with you for like two years. I swear he doesn't understand the words "no" and "I'm married.""

"But that discount is clutch though."

I laugh fully pulling her into a hug.

"Thanks sis. I love you, lock up for me."

Knowing that I've kept him waiting long enough, I take the steps instead of the elevator. I half expect to see him parked outside in a BMW but I'm rather surprised to see him sitting in a black Nissan Pathfinder. It's glowing like new money as if he's just bought it or ran it through a carwash before he came. He sees me and hops out immediately, coming around the front of the car to open the passenger door.

He pauses. "Wow, you look amazing."

I feel my cheeks begin to warm. "Thank you."

He holds the door open for me as I climb inside. He's about as cool as the other side of the pillow as he walks back around, settles himself behind the wheel. He's dressed casually in a black sweater, light blue jeans, and black on black sneakers. I catch a whiff of his cologne as he moves to fasten his seatbelt. If heaven smells like him, I'm in it.

"How was your day?" I ask as he pulls off.

"It was fine. I played a game of basketball with my brother at the civic center, went into the office to catch up on some work, and now I'm here with you."

He smiles at that last part and I have to turn away to hide my own smirk creeping at the corners of my mouth. Unsuccessfully hidden, he notices, asks, "How was yours?"

"Aside from the dress fitting, I spent it with my sister. We did a little shopping, grabbed some lunch, and she kept me company while I got ready."

He nods his head as if intrigued by my mediocre day. Our conversation stops and for the rest of the ride, we are in silence. The only sound is that of a jazz tune permeating from the speakers. I find myself bobbing my head along to its catchy beat. I see him in my peripheral as he looks over at me, laughs to himself obviously amused at my jam session. He turns his eyes back to the road and we continue on to our destination.

| OVERNIGHT GUESTS

Twenty minutes later, he pulls up outside of the restaurant. The young man working valet opens my door politely assisting me out of the car. It is rather fancy and I immediately feel underdressed when we step inside of the dimly lit waiting area.

"Good evening. I have reservations for Grayson Powell."

The hostess runs a long, acrylic nail down the length of the paper in front of her, checks his name off of the list, and grabs two menus escorting us to a table.

He has expensive taste or maybe it's the décor that is drawing the illusion.

"This is beautiful."

He smiles satisfyingly. "I'm glad you like it."

We order margaritas, peruse the menu a few minutes longer then place our food orders with the waitress.

"I know I said this earlier but you really do look great."

His eyes settle on me, his stare magnetic.

"Thank you...again."

I swallow hard. I can't even hide my nervousness if I wanted to. He licks his lips invitingly. He has me about as hot as fish grease right now.

"It's not polite to stare."

He chuckles. "I can't help it."

The waitress arrives with our drinks and I ease with a sigh of relief when he unpins me from his hypnotic glare.

I'm reeling between the states of drunkenness and being tipsy, cruising carefree down the road of tow up. I have only eaten a portion of my food but I have been sucking this drink down like it's going out of style.

I wonder if he's trying to get me drunk.

A million naughty thoughts run through my head as I watch him read over the drink menu; those muscular arms, full lips, and large hands. *My goodness!*

"What's wrong?"

His voice snaps me out of my trance.

"Nothing," I stammer taking a sip from my drink.

He raises an eyebrow at me as if to say, "You're lying." The words never leave his mouth.

He eyes me then my drink, asks, "Would you like another one?"

I'm undecided. He doesn't give me much of a chance to accept or decline before he waves the waitress over.

"I'll order you a small one. If you want it, drink it. If not, leave it."

I frown. "That's a waste of money, don't you think?"

He shrugs. "You can't take it with you."

That's what people with money say.

"My brother asked about you today," he tells me.

"Oh?"

I'm shocked. More, because he remembers who I am even though he was engulfed in his phone during our introduction, than the fact that he actually inquired about me.

"What did he say?"

"He asked me what I thought of you after our *date* last night."

I rest my elbows on the table and lean in, curious. "And you said...?"

He smirks. "I told him I like you."

My eyes fly open, unable to hide my surprise.

"Oh. Is that right?" I blurt out.

Not the least bit phased by my quick tongue, he says coolly, "I like what I see in you so far. Is that a problem, Farah?"

I shake my head no, unable to push the words from my brain out through my mouth. Once again, right on time, the waitress is back shifting his attention.

The warmth that once lingered in the air is gone, now replaced with a cool night's breeze. It's almost ten when we walk out of the restaurant. I see that as I quickly send a text telling Clarissa he is taking me back home. We stand curbside as valet retrieves the car. Though my sweater is rather thick, it is no match against the lashing winds. Grayson puts his arm around me, surprises me as he gathers me in close to him. His body heat is scorching and I am warmed immediately. His truck comes around the corner and the valet boy races around the front of it. Eager to get out of the cold air, Grayson pushes a twenty dollar bill into his hand as he opens the door for me to get in. The heat is blaring and it feels welcoming compared to the cold outside of these four doors.

"Are you okay to drive?" I ask watching him fumble with his seatbelt.

"I don't think you can handle this *big* thing," he says.

It sounds like a challenge yet I can't tell if he's referring to the car or what's resting between his thighs.

"Don't be so sure."

He smirks. "I'm okay, I can drive."

My drunkenness has fully settled in and though my eyes were open the entire time, the ride home seems like a blur. Within the fastest fifteen minutes in drunken folks time, he is pulling his car up to the front of my apartment complex.

"I had fun," he says looking over at me.

I try not to pout like a big damn kid. I don't want the night to end. I ask, "how far do you live from here?"

"About twenty minutes."

I'm misbehaving and I know it as the words escape my lips. "I really don't think you should be driving. You were doing a little swerving on the way here."

I did feel it a time or two, could have been the wind but I go with my theory instead.

He narrows his eyes at me. "Ms. Acosta..."

Quickly, I mumble, "You can sleep on the couch. I just don't want you drinking and driving."

He already did though, my brain responds sarcastically.

His eyes penetrate mine. "Are you going to behave?"

Hell no!

"Of course Mr. Powell, I'll be on my best behavior."

He exhales. "Okay, I'll stay."

I don't even fake the funk, I let my smile show.

"Drive up to the keypad. I'll show you where to park."

I try to keep my composure as best as possible without seeming extremely drunk as I direct Grayson to the nearest visitor parking spot. I put in the code to get in the building or at least I attempt to; one time with failure and the second time with success. Grayson is thoroughly amused as I stagger into the elevator and press the button for the tenth floor repeatedly until the doors creep shut.

"You're drunk," he says with a laugh.

I giggle; cover my mouth with a hand. "I don't know what you're talking about."

Those eyes, they practically undress me as they run from my head down to my feet.

"What did I tell you about staring?"

He runs a hand over his hair, visibly embarrassed that he has been caught.

"If only I could help it."

The elevator comes to a complete stop, eases open granting access to my floor. I fumble my house keys in my hand. I am seeing twelve when there are only four on the whole damn keychain! Inside, the foyer is dark except for a few slivers of light coming through the blinds from the streetlamps illuminating the sidewalk below my window. Feeling around for the hallway light, I fail to see the shoe lying in the floor until I have clumsily tripped over it. Grayson grabs me quickly before my skull can collide with the ground, his arm secured around my waist.

"Okay Ms. Acosta, lets get you in bed."

"Are you coming with me?"

He chuckles. "I thought you said I could sleep on the couch."

My room is still in disarray but I don't have enough stability to move the bras and panties out of sight.

"Sorry for the mess," I announce kicking a shirt out of my way. "Umm...I don't mind if you sleep in here is all I meant."

"I'm not judging and I think it's best I sleep on the couch."

Damn it!

I settle myself on the bed trying feverishly to undo the zipper of my boot. I am unsuccessful.

"I'll help you," he offers grabbing my calf gently as he slowly pulls the zipper down.

His eyes are fixed on me as they have been for most of the night. Gracefully, he pulls off each boot, better than I could have on a sober night. I bite my lip, the sensation of wanting pulsing at the base of my vagina. I grab a handful of his sweater and pull him close to me capturing his lips with my own. I can't help myself, I want him. A groan escapes his throat, his hands in my hair. I reach for his belt. He congeals, draws away from me damn near pulling me off of the bed with him.

"We should go to bed," he pants.

Bed, yes! Lets do that.

"Okay," I reply, my fingers on the hem of my sweater ready to pull it up over my head.

"No," he stammers grabbing my arm. "You sleep in your bed and I'll sleep on the couch."

The record scratches, the party my hormones are having is interrupted by the ain't-getting-none police.

"Grayson…"

"I'm serious, Farah. It's probably not every day that you get turned down by a man as beautiful as you are but I would rather wait."

"I…I…"

"Look—I'm not looking for a woman to just have casual sex with. I have been there, done that…wrote a book about it. I like you and I respect you and I think it's best that we wait…please."

"This is embarrassing," I murmur trying to hide my face with my hands.

Grayson grabs them pulling them down into my lap.

"There's nothing to be embarrassed about," he says comfortingly. "I want it just as much as you do. Trust me, this isn't an easy thing to turn down but I don't want to take it there just yet. You understand right?"

I do but then again I don't. The alcohol is clouding my judgment. At this point, I guess it is best that I just go to bed.

I look up into his face, force a smile and answer, "Yeah, I understand."

He's not convinced but I don't give him a chance to combat me. I am on my feet headed for the hallway closet.

"I'll get you a pillow and blanket."

| Waking Hopes

The sunlight is ignorantly bright seeping through the cracks in the blinds. I groan pulling the comforter over my head. I can feel my head beginning to thump and I quickly remember how embarrassingly my night ended. I wash down two painkillers with a few handfuls of water from the bathroom sink, brush the taste of last night's margaritas from my mouth, and comb my hair out of the bird's nest it's in. Dressed in a tank top and underwear, I wrap my deep purple silk robe around my torso and head into the living room. Apart of me is hoping he has left so I don't have to face him again but I have no such luck as I spot him sprawled out on my cream colored couch.

I tip toe into the kitchen easing open cabinets as I pull coffee and filters out to make a fresh pot. My stomach grumbles and I settle on the idea of making breakfast. I open the refrigerator and pull out a pack of bacon and a carton of eggs, careful as not to stir up too much noise. I manage to chop up some onions, peel a few potatoes and get some coffee brewing without waking him. *He sleeps like a damn log.*

But as soon as the bacon hits the pan, sizzles, he is up stretching loudly. His sweater is off and he is in a white tank top. His broad shoulders and large arms catch my attention. I notice an oversized tattoo on his chest.

"Good morning."

He moves into the kitchen taking a seat at the island. "Good morning, Mr. Powell."

He smiles and I can't help but think how attractive he looks fresh out of sleep.

"I'm sorry to wake you," I reply.

"Don't. It was the bacon that did it. It smells great in here."

I laugh. "Can I get you some coffee? Do you drink it?"

"Yes and yes."

He is quiet but he watches me as I move about the kitchen. It's almost unnerving being the center of his attention. I pour him some coffee; he likes it black with two sugars.

"So what do you normally do on Sundays?" he asks. "Do you lounge around and watch Lifetime like most women?"

"That was cute but no. I spend it with my folks, sister, and her husband normally. We have Sunday dinner."

"Oh," he says but his tone is a bit solemn. I cringe inwardly, I can't imagine life without my parents and I'm almost sorry I even mentioned it.

"Do you have *any* family other than your brother?"

He sips from his mug. "I have an aunt in Ohio. I have seen her only a handful of times since my parents died. My grandparents, both sets, have passed on. The only people I really consider family that I keep in touch with are my Godmother and God sister. They live in Florida so I only see them once in a blue moon."

I'm depressing myself. I change the subject. "What do you do on Sundays? Watch the game, drink beer and eat wings?"

That brings him back to a happier state as he smiles. "You forgot to say pizza too," he teases. "Sometimes I do. I am really a workaholic; I spend most Sundays in my office."

I turn the eye off under the potatoes, they are done. I start to heat the pan to make the eggs.

"It's not good to work all the time. You need some *you* time every once in awhile."

"Too much idle time makes the brain wander. I try my best to avoid that."

I have to constrain myself from prying. My counselor senses want to delve deeper but I can sense that his past holds more than I'm ready for on this beautiful Sunday morning.

"That's understandable."

That is the best response I can give.

I use my key to enter the three story red bricked townhome my parents own just outside of DC. I had lived here for as long as I can remember. Born in New Jersey, the military brought us to the Metro area when I was ten years old. The smell of fried chicken hits me hard when I step into the foyer. My mother was a chef for fifteen years of her life before obtaining a career in real estate. Everything Anita Acosta cooks tastes like she put both feet and her bad knee in it. As always, I stop in the den to see papa before joining the rest of the women in the kitchen.

"There is my little girl!"

His Puerto Rican accent is thick as pie. I don't quite understand how considering he's been in Virginia since his early twenties. My father, known to his daughters as papa, stands to hug me. His height is overbearing, just tall for no reason. Even till this day, I still don't understand why my sister and I are so short considering his stature. He has thick, curly salt and pepper hair with dark grey eyes and a stubble grey beard on his cappuccino colored skin. I always thought I favored papa more than mami.

"Hey papa," I reply wrapping my arms around his waist.

"You look great, baby girl. How are things?"

I smile up at him. "Everything is going well. I really can't complain."

My sister's husband, Christian Davis, is sitting on the worn black leather couch papa refuses to get rid of. His feet propped up on the coffee table which is just as worn out. I peak around papa's large frame and say, "Hey Chris."

He is into the football game blaring from the enormous flat screen television mounted to the wall. Without so much as peeling an eyeball from the tube, he gives me a head nod. Christian is pretty tall too, at least six feet or so. I don't know what it is about the Acosta women attracting these tall men. He's rather stocky with large arms and a protruding midsection. He is bald headed with a face full of facial hair like a damn werewolf. He's like the brother I never had, annoying as ever. I roll my eyes at his lack of a greeting focusing my attention back to papa.

"Your mother told me about this guy you're dating."

I groan. I go on a date and a half and now we're dating.

"It's about time," Christian murmurs.

I hear his snide remark and cut my eyes at him. "I heard that. How about you shut the fuck up over there, eh?"

"Farah!" Papa's voice is demanding and loud.

I cower at his tone. Somehow he forgets he cusses like a sailor too. I am his child; my potty mouth comes from him.

"I'm sorry, he started it. I just met him Friday, we're not dating."

His expression softens and I am back in his good graces.

"He better be treating you appropriately or else..."

I think papa believes he's some mafia man and at a snap of a finger, can make any man disappear. He gives the same empty threat every time.

"I wouldn't stand for it any other way.

"Can you stand to be quiet?" That is Christian again and I instantly wish I had something to throw at him.

I sneer at him, "You know what Chris..."

"Aye you two, cut it out!" Clarissa walks in just in time to stop the world war about to brew between her husband and me. "Retreat to your corners, mami said to come eat."

"You are so damn lucky," I tell Christian through clenched teeth. "It was about to be on like donkey Kong!"

He throws his 220 pound arm weight over my shoulder with a laugh. "Yeah whatever, it's good to see you. I've missed you, sis."

The spread is lavish as it always is. Healthy pieces of fried chicken, a pan of macaroni and cheese, fresh collard greens, and sweet cornbread sit in the middle of the oversized dining room table.

"You have certainly outdone yourself yet again ma," Chris retorts giving a drum stick googly eyes. I'm surprised he isn't salivating at the mouth and sweating butter to go with the cornbread as excited as he is.

"Well thank you sweetheart," mami beams.

"You're such a suck up," I whisper just enough for him to hear.

He shoves me so hard; I fly into a dining chair toppling it over into the floor.

"You're so damn clumsy, Farah," he teases with a devilish smirk on his face.

Clarissa is near tears with laughter.

I'm going to whoop your ass, I mouth.

Papa steps in between us grabbing our hands tightly with stern eyes.

"Since my youngest daughter doesn't know how to act, she's going to say the prayer."

Mami gives me the fakest smile monopoly money can buy from across the table.

"Yes ma'am. Let us bow our heads: Heavenly Father, we come to you today to thank you for all of your blessings despite our sins. Bless the families at this table Lord touching their lives and keeping them out of harm's way. Watch over us as we go about our daily lives this week and give us patience and strength to endure whatever may come our way. Bless the hands that prepared this meal before us and may it be nourishment to our bodies. All of these things I ask in your name, Amen."

"Amen, that was beautiful baby girl," papa says kissing me on my temple.

"Thanks papa."

We take seats at the dining table and dig right in.

I am wrist deep in dishwater. Clarissa is next to me drying the dishes as I hand them to her.

"How was your date last night?"

I can tell the question has been eating away at her curiosity.

I smile a little bit at the thought of him. I do like him; he is very different from any man I have ever met.

"It went well, we had a nice time."

I pause, unsure if I want to tell her about my embarrassing moment. However, this is my sister and I least expect she will judge me.

"What's wrong?" she quizzes as if hearing the gears in my head turning as I think.

I rinse my hands off and dry them with a paper towel. "I kind of did something stupid."

She places the plate in her hand on the counter as if bracing herself for the tale I am about to tell.

"What did you do? Did you have sex with that man?"

Her voice has dropped down to a whisper, her eyes cutting into me wanting me to get on with the juicy stuff.

"No!" I exclaim. "Well...I wanted to but he turned me down. I told him he was too drunk to drive so he would come upstairs. I set up all the pins and he threw me a gutter ball."

She blinks rapidly in confusion. "Is he gay?"

I can't help the laugh that escapes me. "Gosh no...Well, shit I hope not. That would be a travesty. He said he wanted to wait before we took it there."

She leans her widened hip against the counter, folds her arms over her chest. "Well I'll be damned, a true gentleman.

"Is that what it is?"

She flicks the damp towel at me hitting me on the thigh.

"Ow bitch!"

"Farah, listen to you. He could have been like any other man and just hit it and quit it. He didn't and you should actually be happy about that."

I frown. "It seems like it has been forever since...you know. My hormones were going crazy and I...I just embarrassed the hell out of myself."

"I don't doubt it. Well he didn't go running for the hill, that's a good thing. I take it you like him, huh? He seems to really like you."

"I do. I really do."

Clarissa beams. "I can tell. So far it sounds like you've got a good one. He's way better than that asshole you used to date."

"Clarissa Davis!"

She shrugs unapologetically. "I never liked him and you know that Farah. I always said you deserve better and I'm crossing my fingers and toes that this Grayson character just *might* be it."

That would be nice, I think to myself.

I UNEXPECTED GIFTS

I hate Mondays. They come around way too fast, they are the start of the work week, and I always feel like they are the most hectic day of them all.

"Good morning beautiful!"

Cathy Franks greets me as I walk through the double glass doors of the office. She is a pale, slender woman a few years my junior. She has beautiful dark red curls that hang just below her shoulders, her eyes a mix between blue and green. I hired her as the firm's receptionist after Audrey's retirement.

"Hey girl, how was your weekend?" I lean my elbow on the corner of her desk.

"I didn't do shit," she says in a whisper even though it's just she and I in the lobby. "It was a Red Box and red wine type of weekend. How was yours?"

I reply nonchalantly, "I had a date."

She gasps with excitement. "Spill it!"

"His name is Grayson Powell. I met him when I went out with Clarissa and Terri Friday night, we went out Saturday night, he's fine as shit, and I think I like him."

She falls back in her chair, shakes her head at me. "Damn, I'm jealous. I'm happy for you though. Do you think it will lead anywhere?"

I shrug collecting the stack of messages she hands me. "Hell if I know. I hope so, he is a great guy."

"Well, I hope it does, "she says. "You are a good woman and you deserve a great man to compliment you."

I feel all warm and fuzzy on the inside. I blush, say, "Thanks girl, I appreciate that. What you got for me?"

"You have a meeting at ten this morning and one at three. Ms. Frasier had to move her session so it has been rescheduled for tomorrow afternoon. Other than that, your week is looking pretty open."

I groan. "I hate meetings."

Cathy laughs at me. "That's what happens when you're the boss."

I am thankful that my ten o'clock meeting is brief. It's with Audrey to go over the development of the company. I hate to see her now. When I met her she was heavy set with dark olive skin, brown hair, and dark green eyes. She moved to DC from Boston with her now ex-husband some odd years ago. A boisterous Italian woman, she loved to wear her hair tall and stiff with hairspray. Her makeup was always gaudy but she could dress her ass off. Everything down to the case she used to carry her cigarettes in was name brand. When I look at her now, it is as if she's a different person. Her skin has gotten paler, she's at least thirty pounds lighter and her hair is thinning horribly. Her eyes have sunken into her face and she has that raspy, I've-been-smoking-for-too-damn-long voice. She can't even sign her signature without her hands shaking. Graciously, her husband, Mr. Edward Tine, is still supportive and actively involved in the affairs of her business when she is unable to tend to it.

"Everything has been running very well, I see."

"It has."

The rock on her finger is gleaming, the rest of her jewelry looks like it costs more than the lease on my car. I don't want to make myself nauseous thinking about how much that fur coat she has on must have run her. And it's not even *that* cold outside for a fur coat.

I continue, "This year alone, we have counseled over a dozen new families. Many of the counselors, including myself, elect to work from home some days out of the week. Because of this, we conduct more sessions on-site than in office. This has actually increased revenue for us by attracting new clients and increasing sessions with the old. We are definitely moving in a good direction."

Audrey pauses, hacks into a tissue. My stomach turns slightly as she wipes mucus from her lips. "I'm glad I put you in charge. I knew you would be someone beneficial to this firm when you were just an intern."

I smile. "Thanks Audrey."

Mr. Tine is his normal cool self dressed in a crisp white dress shirt and dark grey slacks. He opens up a manila folder, peers at the contents inside then slides it across to table to me.

"The reason for this meeting today is not really about the productivity of this company, Farah," he says. "Don't get me wrong, we are more than satisfied with everything you have done. I and Mrs. Tine have been doing a lot of talking and debating within these last few months. Her health is failing and frankly, if anything happens I don't think I can manage this company on my own."

My heart drops into my lap. Am I being laid off? Is that what he is telling me right now?

"I have my own company," he continues. "And both of them would just be too much to handle at once. We have given it a lot of thought and we believe the best thing to do is sign the company over to you."

"What?" I shout nearly slobbering on my coral colored dress shirt. "I...I...can't accept that."

Audrey reaches for her cup of water sitting on the table. Unable to hold it steady enough to drink, Mr. Tine lifts it to her lips. She swallows loudly, clears her throat, and says, "Your mother is a great friend of mine and she wouldn't have insisted

I bring you on if she wasn't confident in what you could do for this company. You were born a leader, Farah. Look at what you've done in the last year alone."

Words fail her and she stops to gather herself.

"My wife is right," Mr. Tine chimes in. "You've really changed things up for the better and it's really working. This thing started off with two people and look at what it has become. If you don't take it, we'll be forced to sell it. That's the last resort."

I'm in shock. My eyes wide, my mouth gaped. "I couldn't do that to these women," I stammer. "They need these jobs and our clients need us."

"So you'll take it over?" Audrey pushes.

My eyes dart from her to Mr. Tine. I feel like I'm sitting beneath a hot interrogation light about to confess to a murder I didn't commit. *You can do this*, I tell myself. Shit, I've been doing it for the last two years. The only difference is the Tines are no longer my boss; I will be my *own* boss. I finger the documents in the manila folder. They are leases, loan statements, and other things to be signed over to me. I notice the rent on the office has been paid up for the next three years. All I have to do is sign. I walked in here having a meeting with my boss and I'll be walking out like...a boss.

"You don't have to decide today. I know your sister is a lawyer, look over things and make sure of its wording. We need to know by the end of the week just in case we decide to sell."

It's as if Mr. Tine's eyes are pleading with me. He knows his wife won't make it much longer and he needs me to help him. If I do this, my colleagues keep their jobs as well as myself and all the people we help on a daily basis keep their services.

I sigh. "Give me until the end of the day and I'll let you know."

Mr. Tine smiles over at me. He knows I can't let everything I've worked hard for be sold off as just some office space.

"Thank you, Farah."

I take an early lunch, head north toward Clarissa's office. My head is clouded, I feel like my brain is about to explode. Realizing I can't just pop up at her job unannounced, I hit the speed dial on my cell praying silently that she answers.

"Hey Farah."

"Clare, I need some emergency sister time."

"What the hell did he do?" she snaps.

"He? Bitch, what? Oh...nothing. This isn't about Grayson."

She exhales loudly. "Good. What's wrong?"

"Can you see me or not?" I press.

She pauses for a moment, checking her schedule I assume. "I have an hour before my next meeting."

"Perfect, I'll be there in ten."

"Well it all looks pretty good."

I watch her nervously as she sifts through the documents, her reading glasses perched on the edge of her nose.

"I cannot believe you are about to own that company!" she exclaims. "Your hard work did that for you."

Uneasy, I smile. "Do you think I can do it?"

She scuffs. "Farah, are *you* seriously sitting here doubting yourself? We all know what you've poured into that company and it's bigger than it has ever been. Nothing is going to change except the owners, and now that is you. I'm so happy for you sis, I'm really proud. You always said you wanted to own your own firm."

I shake my head still a bit overcome with shock. "I did, didn't I?"

"They keep all of their finances intact, everything is up-to-date. The Tines have always been upstanding people. They've done all of the hard work for you, you just have to accept."

I inhale sharply standing to my feet. "Thanks for seeing me on such short notice to look this over."

Clarissa comes around her desk enveloping me in her arms. "Girl shut up, you're my sister. If you break a nail, I'll rearrange a meeting for you."

I laugh loudly. "I love you."

"Love you too."

I don't have much of an appetite so I skip lunch and head back to the office. I draw the curtains and sit in the dark as I wait for my last meeting cradling a headache that has suddenly come on. My phone vibrates. I smile seeing that I have a missed text from Grayson.

I have been thinking about you all day. I want to see you, when can we make it happen?

For a second, he makes me forget what I'm even stressing about. I text back:

Tonight, I would love to see you tonight. I have had a stressful day. A drink and good company would be great.

He is swift with his reply.

I'll cook dinner since you made breakfast. How about 7:30 tonight at my place. Don't worry about bringing anything except yourself.

I smile widely, tell him:

You just made me an offer that I can't refuse, Mr. Powell. Send me the address; I will see you around 7.

I have thirty more minutes left until my next meeting, I am dreading it. There is a knock at my door before Cathy pushes it open.

"Whoa! Do you need a new light bulb?"

I laugh though I know she is sincerely asking. "No Cathy, I just have a headache."

"Oh girl, cause I was about to say there are plenty of light bulbs in the utility closet. You don't have to sit up in the dark like this." She chuckles at her joke. "Anyway, the director for the last meeting called to cancel."

I say a quick prayer of thanks under my breath. "Thank you...oh, Cathy...can come in here for a minute?"

Hesitantly, she steps inside of the darkened room clinging to the sliver of light coming in through the open door. "You can turn the light on."

She flicks it on illuminating my office once again.

"What's up?" she asks coming to sit in the winged chair that sits in front of my mahogany desk.

"I have some good and bad news that I need to tell you."

Her eyebrows furrow. "Lets start with the bad."

I swallow hard. "Okay. The bad news is I need to hire a new receptionist immediately."

Her expression is melancholy. This is a cruel joke and I speak quickly to get the rest out before she cries, "The good news is I will be taking over ownership of this firm and I would like for you to be my personal assistant."

"Oh my goodness!" she exclaims damn near leaping across my desk to hug me. "Congratulations."

"Thank you," I say with a laugh. "Congratulations are in order for you too."

"When? How?"

"As you can surely tell, Audrey is very sick and they don't know how much longer she will make it with her health deteriorating. Mr. Tine is juggling both businesses now part-time but once she passes, it will be his full responsibility. He can't manage so they are signing the firm over to me. I decided to accept."

She presses me to her in a tight hug. "Really? This is so amazing. I'm so happy for you. You have done amazing things with this company so far."

"Thank you Cathy, that means a lot. But look, I need you to compose a job ad for a receptionist before you leave, email it to me for final approval. I need a new girl by the end of the week and you can take over the office across the hall."

Cathy squeals animatedly. "Thank you, Farah!"

I throw my arm over her shoulders. "I wouldn't dare choose another gal over you. Besides, who else is going to be the Ivory to my Ebony?"

And we laugh heartily.

I Naked Games

Twenty five minutes, two u-turns, and some faulty ass directions later, I turn into Grayson's quaint community. Darkness has rested over the city and it seems as though everyone has settled in for the night aside from the two couples I spot walking their dogs around the neighborhood. With little trouble, I find his house pulling into the driveway behind his truck. I turn the car off and climb out at exactly seven-thirty. I would have arrived sooner if I didn't over sleep the three hour nap I caught at the office. I double check the number of the house to make sure it's correct before knocking. He doesn't keep me waiting long. The door swings open after a minute and

Grayson is on the other side dressed in a plain black t-shirt, grey sweatpants with bare feet.

"Hey beautiful."

His voice, his smile, his whole presence is enough to make my entire day feel less crazy. He steps to the side giving me space to come in.

"Hi," I say shyly as though we are meeting again for the first time.

He takes me by surprise when he bends down and kisses me. I reach up; run my thumb across his lips to remove the lip gloss I have left behind.

He smiles, says, "It slipped my mind to ask if you ate seafood but then I remembered you were eating a salmon salad at the restaurant Friday night."

I pause, look up at him. "Someone pays close attention."

"I've noticed a lot of things about you, Ms. Acosta. Come."

He grabs my hand pulling me into the kitchen. It is oversized with wooden floors and beautiful gradient countertops. All of the appliances are stainless steel including the refrigerator which has a see-through door. He opens it pulling out a bottle of red wine, Merlot. I don't recognize the label as a brand I have tried before. At this moment, I don't give a damn. I just need a drink.

Red wine, another thing he noticed about me that night.

Reading my puzzled expression as my eyes scan the label, he says, "I asked my Godmother about red wines. She has a wine cellar and she drinks nothing but it. She said this was the best one."

"It looks expensive."

He ignores me reaching in a cabinet for two wine glasses. "I'll pour us a glass and take you on a tour."

He uses some fancy contraption to open the bottle and pours us both a glass of the red liquid.

"Mm, it is yummy."

Hesitant, he takes a sip, frowns.

"You don't have to drink it for me," I say with a chuckle.

Hurriedly, he sets the glass back on the counter. "Good, you can have that then."

I'm flattered at the fact that he even attempted to drink it off the strength of me. He pulls open the fridge again, this time retrieving a beer.

"This is more my speed," he replies before taking a swig.

He grabs my hand again leading me back out into the foyer, down a short hallway and into the living room. It's painted a rich, deep red color and the art lining the walls are all in black and white. It's cozy in here. There is a plush black couch decorated with red and black throw pillows. There are two rounded glass top end tables with curved bases. The coffee table is similar, only larger. It smells heavenly in here, a mix of Jasmine and pine trees, somewhat manly. He has a large entertainment system with a giant flat screen television and a state of the art stereo that looks as if I would need the instruction manual to find the on button. My size seven feet sink into the posh cream carpet as we move through to a door sitting off the corner of the living room. The door reaches from floor to ceiling and on the other side is a large office space with a huge blueprint table on one side and an oversized cherry oak desk on the other. It's also painted the same color red as the living room. He has two armchairs that sit in front of the desk.

Maybe he has clients that come here, I think.

He takes me to the dining room next which is half the size of the other two rooms I've seen. It is a nice brown color that makes the cherry oak dining table and chairs stand out. It has minimal decorations aside from the large painting that hangs on the wall adjacent the table and a big plant sitting off in a corner. There's a half bath downstairs that looks as though it is rarely used. Upstairs, he takes me into the master bedroom. *Holy shit*, I think to myself when the first thing I see is a king size bed. I make a mental note that red must be his favorite color. The bed is made up of red sheets and a black and white comforter. There's a large red circular rug in the middle of the bedroom floor. The nightstands and entertainment system are all black. His closet is the size of his office damn near. The clothes are neatly hung and his shoes are lined perfectly in its only little section. I can only imagine what his paychecks must look like! His master bathroom is nauseatingly big with a whirlpool tub that is separated off from the walk-in shower with *two* showerheads. He has his and her sinks and I eye his collection of colognes placed ever so neatly on the counter. *He's got good taste.* There's a second bedroom with a queen size bed and a dresser. It has a bathroom that is connected. They are both plain and not as lavishly decorated as the rest of the house. I assume it is only due to it being just him.

"This place is really something," I gush gripping his hand as he leads me back downstairs.

"Thank you. This is my kingdom, my greatest purchase."

"And you decorated this?" I ask with a raised eyebrow.

He laughs reaching out to push a hair from my face, tucking it behind my ear. "Are you kidding me? I can barely separate my clothes properly let alone decorate a place like *this*. My God sister is an interior decorator; all credit is due to her."

I breathe a sigh of relief. At least he didn't say an ex-girlfriend did it.

"Are you hungry?"

He licks his lips as he asks me this and I am immediately thrown off. Are we talking food or...?

I settle with the safer response and reply, "I'm starving."

I'm sitting in front of a spread of seafood pasta and fresh Caesar salad, across from an attractive man that is staring at me like he is trying to commit my face to memory.

"Why are you always staring at me?" I ask winding a spoonful of the creamy pasta around my fork. It's delicious and yet again I'm impressed that he is fine, keeps a neat home, and can cook.

"You're beautiful and I can't help it. I have told you that."

I hide my lips with a napkin until I have swallowed my mouthful of food. "Thank you."

He takes a swig from his beer. "You said your day was stressful, what happened?"

I drink from my glass of wine. It really is good and I tell myself I need to get a bottle of this soon.

"I...um...took ownership of the counseling firm today."

He sulks at me as if to say, "You're crazy if that's stressful."

I answer him before he can ask. "I became manager two years ago when the boss had a stroke and retired. I've been running it for the last two years but the thought of having to handle *everything* is a little unnerving."

"I see." I hate when people say I see because they don't *really* see anything, they just don't have shit else to say. "It's probably not as bad as you think it will be; nonetheless, congratulations are in order."

"Thank you, I appreciate it."

"How is the food?"

"It's delicious," I say sucking up a noodle while eyeing him.

He smirks at my playfulness. "I'm glad you like it."

Behave Farah.

"You don't get lonely in this big ole house?"

He looks around at the bare walls of the dining room, his gaze sets on the picture and then on me. "Wouldn't anyone?"

"Why aren't you married?" I halfway don't mean to ask it, at least not so soon but it's already out of my mouth and I am curious for the answer.

"I haven't asked you yet."

My eyes widen. He chortles at my expression, "I'm kidding! Relax Farah. I...uh...had a really bad break up a few years ago. I'm just taking things slow with whoever comes into my life. Do you not think that you will make a great owner of *your* company?"

We are back on the subject. My company, it seems like foreign language.

"I don't know what to think," I admit. "I'm over thinking, this I know."

"Do you always over think?"

My tone sultry, the wine is sinking in. I answer, "Yes. I almost feel as though I can't help not to. It's a bad habit."

"Properly noted, Ms. Acosta."

His gaze settles over me, this is becoming a regular thing with him. The attraction, the electricity is strong between us. I'm only halfway done with my food but I leap to my feet, he has me disoriented.

"I'll take the dishes to the kitchen," I stammer.

"Sit. You're not even done with your food."

Shit, I cuss to myself sinking back down into the chair. I press my legs tightly together trying desperately not to soak my panties with my wetness.

"I don't take you as the nervous type, Farah. Do I make you nervous?"

Ok, if you're going to play this game Grayson, I'll join you. "No, you just turn me on."

I don't even know myself in this moment but I grin devilishly on the inside at his expression. His mouth is hung open with surprise. He tries to maintain his cool, says, "Do I?"

I'm not good at games! He's not playing fair, not by far but I feel like I can beat him at his own match. I pull my dress shirt out of the waistband of my pencil skirt; undo the first two buttons all while keeping my eyes fixed on him. This time, he can't keep his eyes steady as they trail down to my breasts.

"It's hot," I say snatching his attention back.

He clears his throat, runs a hand over his head. "It is a little bit warm in here."

"You seem a bit nervous yourself, Mr. Powell."

"I suppose you might be rubbing off on me."

"Do you always play games like this?"

He shifts in his seat, clears his throat. "I wouldn't call it playing games, more like flirting."

It's too much conversation going on. I'm ready to leap across this table and have my way with him. He smirks a little and my inner woman screams loudly, frustrated. So I get up, instead of taking control. I walk out. Out into the foyer where my purse is sitting on the table in the hall, my heels moving noisily against the hardwood floor.

"Farah," I hear him say after me. I would have made it out of the door had I not dropped my phone before I can manage to get it open.

"Shit!" I bend down scooping it up; stuff it into my purse without checking to see if the screen is broken. He grabs my arm gently but firmly turning me around to face him.

I have some choice words for him. I plan on serving him every piece of my mind but before the words can leave my mouth, he kisses me. He presses my body between him and the door, our lips tangled in a passionate kiss. I push him away with all the might I can muster. Why? I'm not really sure.

"This is amusing to you, huh?"

My lips are raw from our kisses.

"I'm trying my damndest not to touch you," he breathes. "You have no idea how hard it is for me not to want to feel every inch of you under my fingertips. And damn if I don't want to be inside of you."

Oh my damn!

"Nobody is stopping you. I thought it was obvious that I want you too."

He grasps my jaw in his hand igniting my flesh with his touch, his lips back on mine. "Shh," he demands against my mouth.

He grabs my purse and tosses it back on the table; the contents spill out against the hard surface. He grabs the edge of my skirt hiking it up to the middle of my thighs, wraps one arm around my waist and the other under my behind. Effortless, he sweeps me up off of the floor forcing my legs around his waist. Barely looking, he carries me up the steps to his bedroom.

My back sinks down onto the pillow top mattress on his bed. For a moment, I feel like a fish out of water trying to pull myself up to a sitting position. He eases my heels off and into the floor. They make a loud thud as they hit the carpet and tumble a few inches away. "Those are Jessica Simpson, easy there."

He smiles fully and for the first time I notice a dimple in his right cheek. It makes him look even sexier, and now I want him that much more. "Fuck Jessica Simpson."

I reach up grabbing him by the nape of his neck, pulling him down into another tug of lips.

"No," I pant in between kisses. "Fuck *me*."

His nerves have got the best of him as he fumbles to drag my stockings down over my hips and thighs. His thick finger tears through the fabric but he continues on as if unnoticed. "These are Jessica Simpson too," I state flexing my toes so he can pull them off.

He laughs. "I'll buy you some new ones. Turn over."

I do as I'm told lying flat on my stomach as he works the zipper to my skirt down and over my backside until its undone enough to be pulled off. I'm in my panties now, black lace panties that don't quite cover my enormous behind. His large hands run over it gripping, groping along the way. He slaps the left one roughly and my skin stings from the lash, pleasurable. He pulls at my waist again and I turn around once more until I'm on my back. We work jointly at the buttons of my shirt, slowly and teasingly. I shrug out of the thin fabric tossing it in the floor somewhere out of sight. He grabs the hem of his shirt yanking it up and over his head. It takes him all of a second to come out of his sweatpants. And now we are both before each other in our underwear, uncensored. I reach for him but he pulls away.

"Wait...just a second. I just want to say something to you before we do *this*."

I feel like he is about to lecture me.

Who the hell gives a disclaimer before sex?

But I channel my attention and listen.

"I like you and...I hope this is not it...you know, I don't want you to think that sex is all I want. I've tried to hold out but I'm drawn to you and...I just don't want to ruin the possibility of a good thing."

I just want to know what part of heaven he's fallen from and do they make others like him there. I reach up and caress his face gently, reassuringly. "You won't."

And when he kisses me this time, it's the most sensual kiss I have ever felt. It's meaningful and I know he is comfortable with me. Strategically, his fingers work against the hook of my bra until it is undone, sliding the straps down my arms. He pauses; steps back to admire my unclothed body.

"I can't get over how beautiful you are to me."

I blush but he doesn't see it, his lips are on my neck working diligently down to the breasts. My nipples harden underneath the touch of his tongue, protrudes at his command. Firmly yet gently, he pushes me back against the mattress as his lips continue its journey. Down farther, past my belly button. Down until they are kissing the tops of my thighs. His fingers dance along the waist of my panties tugging them down over my behind, my hips and into the floor. Small kisses against the insides of my thighs send my body reeling into a near convulsion. It has been months since I have last been intimate with someone; I can barely withstand this teasing. He scoops his arms underneath my thighs prying them apart, yanking me down lower on the bed where my southern lips meet his. I feel his warm breath and then his tongue. *Sweet baby Jesus! Glory!* He licks and sucks relentlessly until I come crashing down around him, my body erupting into a mind blowing orgasm. I buck beneath him, which only makes him tighten his grip.

"Okay!" I holler trying desperately to push his face away.

He laughs sinisterly moving up to kiss me, forcing me to taste myself still lingering on his lips. He reaches in his nightstand and pulls out a condom. My eyes bulge at the length of him, commanding and fully erect. He climbs over me smothering me with his body weight, suffocating me with his heat. I feel his erection at the entrance of my vagina. Little by little, he pushes through to my center. I dig my nails into the skin of his back. He is a lot to take in and my body is ill prepared.

"I'm sorry," he whispers in my ear stilling, giving me the chance to get acclimated to his size.

I say nothing, he continues slowly. And when I have taken the length of him, he moves in a steady pace igniting the flame deep within the pit of my stomach. I raise my hips to meet his thrusts and the feeling is sensational. His teeth sink into the flesh of my shoulder as he speeds to a faster pace.

"Ah!" I wrap my arms around his shoulders pulling him in closer to me, inviting him in deeper. I can feel the familiar friction building up, my legs stiffen and I lose all composure around him. He pounds into me rapidly until his own orgasm is released. He plants soft kisses on my nose and the corners of my mouth, he's gentler than I imagined him to be. I struggle against the heaviness of my eyelids.

"Lets go to bed," he says freeing me from the constraints of his weight.

By the time he empties the used condom in the trash and returns back to my side, I have already succumbed to sleep.

I Happy

It's only Tuesday yet my body feels worn down. I am naked beneath Grayson's sheets, alone. His spot is empty, cold like he has been gone a long time. I sit up quickly scanning the room for signs of him. I spot a pair of dress slacks and a shirt hanging on the door of his closet, and then I hear the shower running faintly from the bathroom. I don't have the energy to move. I'm tired, so very tired. I glance over; his alarm clock reads seven-thirty. Mentally, I try the measure the amount of time it will take me to get up, redress, make it home to change for work, and get to the office on time. I quickly dismiss it settling on the fact that there's no way I can do it especially considering I don't want to move right now. I need to call Cathy but my phone is downstairs in my purse, probably dead as a doorknob. The bathroom door eases open and a wet Grayson emerges with a beige towel wrapped around his waist. I can't help but watch him as he yanks it off, dries the remainder of his body.

"Good morning."

I smile sleepily. "Good morning."

Bare ass, dick swinging he steps back into the bathroom and returns with a bottle of lotion. Again, I stalk his every move as he quickly rubs a few handfuls of into his skin before putting on his underwear.

"You look exhausted, go back to bed."

Back to bed! As in his bed? I look on in confusion, reply, "But you are about to leave for work."

"Wow, you noticed, huh?"

"You know what I meant," I murmur.

He eases one leg at a time into his black dress pants, adjusts his member comfortably, and zips them up.

"I don't know what kind of guys you have dealt with Farah but a *man* such as me is not going to make you leave if you don't have to. What are you going to do? Carry my furniture out on your back? Load it up into your little ass car?"

I am wounded by his words. It makes me second guess the men I have allowed in my life since Calvin. The many mornings I have had to climb out of bed, dead tired and drive home. Embarrassingly, sometimes right after we've committed the act of sin.

"I get it, Grayson. I was just saying."

"If I felt like you were the type of woman to run my pockets while I'm gone, I would have told you to get up and get dressed by now. Did you hear nothing I said to you last night?"

Would that have been before or after the hair pulling?

He exhales loudly, continues, "Stay if you want to stay, go if you feel you have to."

"I heard you. I just...well...I don't know. Forgive me for sounding small minded."

"You have been forgiven, don't do it again."

I giggle. "Yes sir."

"You make me want to get back in the bed...wake you up."

I smirk. "What's stopping you?"

"A 9AM meeting with a contractor for a new project. Believe me, if there wasn't a good reason I would be having *you* for breakfast by now."

I hide my blush with the comforter. I replay last night in my head; the thought of him stirs me alive. I don't feel so tired anymore.

He secures his extravagant timepiece around his wrist, glances at it to check the time. "Let me get going."

I yawn. "Can you bring my purse up before you leave?"

He's adjusting his tie in the dresser mirror. "Yes, I can do that for you."

I watch him a little bit longer while he puts on his suit jacket, sprays a few pumps of cologne on his collar and wrists. I even manage to keep my eyes at bay as he goes downstairs to bring me my phone. Luckily, the battery still has some charge and I send Cathy a text message that I will be in the office in time for my session with Ms. Frasier. I'm back in the clutch of sleep before she can respond.

"How long are you going to keep this up, Cynthia?"

I am staring into the eyes of Cynthia Frasier as she sits in the winged chair crosswise from me, her arms crossed over the beestings she calls breasts. It is three o'clock, I'm well rested. I slept until shortly after twelve. Grayson's bed is like a prison and my body could not break free. I find some printer paper in his office, scribble him a note and leave it on his pillow before seeing myself out. I manage to make it to the office by two-thirty to prepare for my session with Cynthia. Now here we are staring at one another and she is not a happy camper. Ms. Frasier took Cynthia to the abortion clinic last week after finding out that she was pregnant during a routine doctor's visit. She hasn't spoken to her mother since.

"For as long as I feel like it," she mumbles.

"Cynthia, you can't possibly understand the decisions that a mother must make to protect her child. Even if you had a child of your own, you're too young to know. You would be forcing your mother not only to take care of you but your baby as well. That's not fair. Do you really believe you would have been ready for a child?"

She shrugs. "I don't know."

"When kids are involved, the answer can never be I don't know. Children are a serious matter, Cynthia. I'll be honest with you: I don't like abortion either, however, I think what your mother did was necessary. You have so much ahead of you and you need to grow up before you try to mother a child. I know practicing having kids can be a fun thing but the consequences, not so much. I can't sit here and force you to talk to your mother but at least think about what your future might have been like if you brought a child into this world at 14."

Her expression softens and for the first time since Cynthia has been my client, I see tears swelling in her eyes.

"Do you have children, Ms. Acosta?"

"No, Cynthia. I don't have any."

She wipes away a silent tear with the back of her hand. "So how do you know what's the best decision for a mother?"

Damn it, she got me!

"You're absolutely right Cynthia. What in the world do I know? I know that as a woman, if I was in your mother's shoes, I would have done the same thing. I've seen more years of my life than you have and I don't know what on earth I would have done if I would have had a child during some of those periods in my life. I can only imagine how difficult it would be for you. You'll never know what it means to truly be a teenager. You're going to be forced to grow up before you're ready. Don't push the world on yourself before it's time. Trust me; it's so difficult being an adult and I don't have children. I want you to make the most of your life and then have children with a man who loves you for everything you're about. One day, and I know it won't be any time soon, you'll thank your mother for all she's done for you including the abortion."

Cynthia stares at me for a few moments, utters, "Maybe."

A knock at the door halts our heart to heart moment. "Come in," I call out to the person on the other end.

Cathy pokes her head inside the door. "I'm sorry to interrupt, Ms. Frasier asked me to come see if you were ready for her."

I'm pretty sure the woman is in the lobby losing her damn mind, probably pacing the floors and everything.

"Um...yes, give me a few more minutes and I'll be out to get her."

Cathy nods with understanding before closing the door behind her.

"Is there anything else you would like to talk about Cynthia? You know I'm all ears."

"My mom is sending me away in a few weeks," she says, her voice cracking under her words. "I think I'm kind of happy."

I wasn't expecting that. I at least assumed she would be clawing at the floorboards trying not to be shipped off. "Is that right?"

"Yeah, my uncle is pretty cool and being the only child kind of sucks. At least I can be around my cousins now."

I make a few notes in my pad. "You know things are really going to change for you. You can't do the things you've been doing."

She nods. "I know. Maybe things will be better for me in Texas."

"I hate that it had to come to this but I truly hope this move will bring great changes for you."

She smiles and it seems like more of a shock to her that she is smiling than it is to me.

"We still have one more session before you leave but I want you to do one thing for me..."

"What's that Ms. Acosta?"

"Talk to your mother. You're going to be miles and miles away from her. You never know what may happen, don't leave without getting everything out on the table and mending things. Please, for me."

She sighs heavily. "Ok."

It is music to my ears. "I'm going to speak to your mom for a few minutes and schedule our last session. I ordered some sandwiches for lunch; I'll get Cathy to take you to the break room so you can get something to eat."

I step around the desk to make my way to the door. Cynthia wraps her arms around my waist. "I hope you have children someday Ms. Acosta. That would be neat, you're pretty cool."

I hope my children think that someday too. "Thank you Cynthia."

She shuffles nervously in front of me and I desperately want to tell her ass to be still! Her resume tells me her name is Erin Welling and she's been doing receptionist work for the last five years. She is a cute girl. She is short in stature with a rich mocha skin tone, looks like she is all of twenty years old even though she insists she will be twenty-seven next week. Her hair is cut short on one side and long on the other. The side that is long is curled falling perfectly around her face. Her resume is impressive, far better than the other three women I've interviewed today. Cathy is sitting beside me scanning over her resume, same as I.

"Why do you want to leave your current job?" I ask noticing that she is a legal secretary for a big named attorney's office in DC.

She wipes her palms on her brown skirt, clears her throat nervously, "I am going back to school for counseling and...well, I figured I should be in the environment to get some type of exposure of what to expect."

"But you have a great job now. You will gain experience through internships. I'm sure they are paying you more than I am offering."

I gaze at her through unconvinced grey eyes.

"I have always wanted to work here," she mumbles.

I am puzzled; we haven't had an opening at this firm in two years. "I'm sorry Erin, can you explain?"

Her eyes shuffle from me to Cathy. "I remember when you were just an intern here, Ms. Acosta. I was a client, my mother and I. Mrs. Tine was my counselor after being raped by my mother's husband."

She pauses, swallows hard. I don't recall her face but what she is saying must be true, how else would she know I was an intern then.

Remaining professional, I ask, "I would think that you being a former client would turn you off from working here. I am surprised you wanted to step foot in this place again let alone become an employee."

She smiles warmly. "Mrs. Tine was an amazing counselor and she did so much for me. She helped me and I want to be of help in return. Even though...um, I would be getting paid for it."

"I understand. Bare with me for a moment, okay."

She nods as I pull up our client database and type in her name. Just as she says, her name and photo ID pop up. She looks no different now than she did then. I look over at Cathy who nods approvingly.

"If you were to be hired, Ms. Welling, when could you start?"

"Today."

"You don't have to give notice to your current employer?"

"Yes ma'am but I would use the weeks of vacation time I have accumulated to carry me through my two weeks, if that makes sense."

She seems timid, speaks softly like a child but I like her demeanor.

"It makes sense Ms. Welling."

I stand to my feet, smooth out my skirt and look over at Cathy once more before saying, "I hope to see you Thursday morning, Ms. Welling. Welcome to the team."

She smiles so hard; her lips almost crack under its pressure. "Thank you so much, Ms. Acosta. Really, thank you!"

I move around the front of the desk to hug her. "Just show me that you want to be here, that's all I ask."

"I do...I mean, I will. Thank you."

And I feel accomplished. I've made two people happy in one day.

| WEDDING GUESTS

"I think you should invite him to the wedding, I mean it's not too late to bring a date."

"What?" I holler, bewildered.

Terri, Clarissa, and I are sitting around my living room; each of us cradling wine glasses filled with a sweet red wine I purchased from the supermarket the day before. It has been nearly two months since Grayson and I started seeing each other, not sure if it's appropriate to call it dating yet. He's been just as amazing now as the first day I met him. No matter how incredible he has been, it's still early in the game and I am a little befuddled at the thought of him being my date to my best friend's wedding.

"Or not," Terri says with a laugh. "I mean, damn Farah. You have been hiding the man from us. The way he has you glowing these days, you shouldn't even mind bringing him."

I roll my eyes in accordance. "You've met the man one time and you want him to come to your wedding?"

She takes a sip from her glass gingerly, "if he's good enough for my best friend, he's good enough to come to my wedding."

I groan loudly, Terri is adamant. "Fine, I'll tell him but don't be mad if he can't come on such short notice. It is like next week, you know."

"No worries just make sure you tell him."

"Okay bitch, I'll tell him, geez. Happy?"

She grins. "Very."

My tires crunch over the melting snow from last week's snowstorm. I hate winter. I hate driving in the snow. Hell, I can't stand cold weather in general. I want it to be spring again where I don't have to run outside every morning to warm my car up before I leave for work. I turn into Grayson's driveway parking behind his truck as I normally do. I don't wait to knock following instructions from his earlier text message to come right on in.

His home feels so warm and cozy. I ditch my wet *Ugg* boots in the foyer, hang my coat and scarf in the wool closet by the door. A beautiful Jazz song soars from the stereo in the living room; I follow the melody down the hall. Grayson is in his office, hovering over a blueprint propped up on the drafting table. He seems flustered with his face frowned up. He lifts his head noticing me, smiles. "Hey baby."

"You should have told me you were busy," I reply stepping further inside. "I could have waited to see you."

He tosses a thick pencil on the table, walks over to me. "And miss the chance of seeing you? No, I'm good on that."

He kisses me fully, pulls me close burying his face in my neck.

"You smell great," he says.

He trails kisses across my collar and over my jaw line. I moan from the feeling. He presses his body close to me thrusting his erection against my hip. He doesn't give me the chance to speak; he takes my hand in his leading me out into the living room. The tune has changed, it's familiar. I don't know the name but I've heard it before, a song by Nina Simone. He pulls me over to the space in front of the fireplace, proceeds to undress me from my jeans and long sleeve shirt. Once I'm in my bra and panties, he works out of his basketball shorts and t-shirt.

"I missed you," he groans, his lips against my skin.

I gasp at the feel of his fingertips against my thighs as he pushes my panties down into the floor. I ditch my bra so I am completely naked before him. His penis is fully erect and I find myself panting with wanting. We occupy a spot on the floor, my back pressed against the carpet. He eases inside of me, buries himself deep in my back. It has become easier and my body immediately welcomes him.

He grunts loudly in my ear, pushing and pulling inside of me. I clench my eyes tightly blocking out the light in the room, savoring the feeling.

"Oh...Grayson," I whimper feeling my orgasm charging up to be released. He moves faster, the sounds of our flesh colliding overpowers the music that plays around us. I tighten my legs around his waist, bracing myself as a ripple of pleasure pulsates through me beckoning his orgasm to join in. He comes loudly, cussing and calling my name.

We are butt naked. The heat from the fireplace radiates against my skin soothingly.

"I need to ask you something," I say softly.

I'm nervous and I'm not really sure why. It's not like *we're* getting married. I wiggle against him at the feel of my hair tickling my back. He chuckles under his breath sweeping my long curls to one side away from my skin.

"What is it?"

I pull up onto my elbows so I can look him in the eyes. "Will you be my date for my best friend's wedding?"

He tries to hide his surprise but it's noticeable. "She asked me to tell you, she wants you to come, "I speak up immediately trying to ease over the awkwardness.

His fingers play in my hair, he's just looking at me. I'm impatient; I let a minute go by before speaking, "Are you going to say something?"

"People don't just take any ole body to a wedding as their date. She doesn't even know me to want me there."

Hell, I don't know you all that well and I kind of want you there.

"I told her that but she insisted. She likes what you do to me; she says you've been keeping a smile on my face."

That makes him smile. "Have I?"

I smirk. "You haven't noticed?"

"Just thought you've been in a good mood lately, didn't think it was due to me. I might have been hoping I had something to do with it though."

I bend down and kiss him. "Will you go, for me?"

He rolls over pinning me beneath him, his hands resting over my head. "I'll go...only if you let me have my way with you again."

Breathy, I moan, "Mm, yes."

And I feel him coming alive.

| Distance

I have never seen my best friend look as beautiful as she does now. Not to say that she looks a mess any other time but today, today is different. Today I am watching her exchange lifelong vows with the man she loves dressed elegantly in an off-white gown with beautifully embroidered lace around the top. She is practically glowing; eyes filled with tears of happiness. I am not composed clenching a tear dampened tissue in my hands as I try to hold both her bouquet and mine steadily. In the sea of eyes is a man looking at me, wanting me, and crazy enough I want him too. The preacher announces them husband and wife and they kiss with a feverish passion.

Raymond whisks her away down the aisle and out of the church. It's the most romantic thing I've witnessed in a long time.

The reception is booming with all of her family and friends. The DJ is going off on the 1s and 2s. Anxiously, I sit through Raymond and Terri's first dance and a few announcements before the food is prayed over. No sooner has her mother said "Amen"; I am on my feet in search of Grayson. What I'm feeling is crazy. I have gone a whole two days without seeing him and I feel like I'm going to lose it if I don't have him in my presence soon. I want to touch him, to kiss him. I can't believe how much I've missed being with him. It's insane. He's sitting next to Christian engaged in conversation, I find it's about last night's game when I get close enough to hear.

"Everything he is saying is a lie," I state disrupting their conversation.

Christian's eyes fly in my direction, he smiles. "Hey sis, you actually look nice when you've taken a shower."

"And you never do," I joke.

He gives me the middle finger just as Grayson stands from his seat. "You look stunning," he whispers wasting no time kissing me.

I grab the nape of his neck deepening our kiss. It catches him off guard; he clings to me as I move in closer. He breaks away from my lips gasping for his air back.

"I think someone missed me," he pants.

My grey eyes are blazing. My hormones are doing triple mounts, cartwheels, and round-offs all through my body. "I did, very much," I reply unashamed. "I'm sorry."

The DJ spins another record as guests begin to line up at the buffet to get their food. Grayson grabs my hand pulling me out into the lobby of the banquet hall. Once we are away from the noise, he turns to me and says, "Stop apologizing to me, Farah. It's okay to miss me, I missed you too."

"I don't want to come off clingy or overstepping what isn't really there..."

"Farah, for goodness sake, shut up!"

And I do, I don't utter another word.

"If I felt like you were being the least bit clingy, I would have backed off or said something." He pauses long enough to let a mother and daughter get out of earshot as they pass through to the bathroom.

He continues, "I said this to you before, I *really* like you. Be you, act normal because I like it baby. Don't apologize for being you."

"Okay," I say faintly, my emotions are getting the best of me.

He leans down and kisses me. "I should go say congratulations to your friend since she *insisted* I be here."

I giggle; link my fingers through his and we walk back inside hand in hand.

I HAPPY BIRTHDAY

"Girl I would kill to have your curves!" Terri gawks at me as I turn from side to side examining my body in her full length mirror. It's my twenty ninth birthday and I am dressed and ready to dance the night away with my close friends and family. We've all gathered at Terri's house to get dressed and have a few drinks before heading out. I'm wearing a tight black number that reaches slightly above my knee. It's backless stopping just above my butt. I'm feeling like a vixen in my red Jessica Simpson pumps. One thing I am famous for is my extensive collection of JS shoes. It's like she made them especially for my short ass. I run my hands over my curves. I must admit I have been filling out a lot lately. My hips have widened and I swear my butt is getting bigger.

I've got to lay off the sex, I say to myself with a laugh.

"Grayson is going to tell you to march right back upstairs and change out of that dress, missy."

Clarissa comes up behind me and jiggles the cuff of my behind. "Where the hell did this come from?"

I swat her hand away, blushing. "Don't worry about it."

Terri pokes, "Grayson's been tapping that ass, that's where it came from."

I laugh heartily. "Forget both of you. Nobody is talking about all that ass you got back there Clarissa."

She sticks her tongue out in my direction.

"And I'm not wearing that tight ass dress either."

Ignoring them, I turn my attention back to the mirror. I apply one more coat of red lipstick, run a hand over the bun sitting perfectly atop my head and tuck my clutch under my arm.

"Lets go already, I want a drink."

"Girl, I'm telling you," Terri says as we head for the steps. "You're looking really good in that there dress. It's about to be a problem when we get in this club. Grayson might have to put you on a leash."

I gracefully walk down the steps behind Clarissa where the fellas are waiting on us, Christian, Raymond, Grayson, and his brother Elliott. It has been forever since I have been out, let alone to the club. I begin to second guess if what I have on is too much. I quickly dismiss the idea. As long as it took me to squeeze my behind in this dress, I am not changing. The men are holding shot glasses in the air when we walk in. They throw their shots back, all except Grayson. He's staring at me, mesmerized by me and I'm naked under his gaze.

"Wow, Farah you look amazing." Elliott gives me a once over quickly trying hard not to stare.

Christian chimes in, "Yeah sis, I can't even pick with you. You look great."

I'm shocked. It's rare Christian doesn't have a snide remark for me.

"Well geez babe, how the hell do I look?" Clarissa folds her arms over her chest tapping her foot at Christian.

He pulls her in close, kisses her on the cheek. "She'll be ugly again tomorrow babe and you will still be cute."

She laughs and I can't help but to laugh too. I spoke too soon.

The electricity behind Grayson's stare is pulling me in his direction. His eyes follow me until I'm standing in front of him; close enough to smell the liquor lingering on his breath. I feel as though the room is watching him as he reaches behind me and runs his finger down my bare back. He opens his palm running his hand over my ass cupping the meaty part of my thigh underneath.

"Is this what I'm going to have to deal with all night?" he asks with a grin.

His stare makes me feel like the whole world is looking at me. Even when I feel like I am the center of attention, no one except Grayson is paying me any mind. "What do you mean?"

"I mean everyone looking at you, *staring* at you."

"The way you're doing now..."

My body tightens as his free hand moves up the fabric of my dress, touching the bare flesh between my legs. "No panties."

"Not in this dress," I breathe wiggling away from his fingers. I bridge space between us reaching to grab the bottle of Hennessey and pour myself a shot.

He licks his lips seductively, his eyes low from drinking. He holds his shot glass up again, clinks it with mine, and we drink. In the eleven months I've been with this man, he knows all the ways to undo me without so much as laying a hand on my body. I can't believe it will be a year next month. *My, how time flies.* We aren't official but I want to be. We haven't talked much about it, merely enjoying the excitement of each other I suppose. He's been around my sister numerous times and despite mami's nagging, I can't bring myself to introduce him to my parents.

"Please stop looking at me like that," I plead putting a playful hand over his eyes.

He chuckles. "We should go before we don't make it anywhere."

I take two more shots before we leave the house. I stagger a little as I get in the car and I know it's going to be a great night.

The three shots have crept up on a sister. I am not quite drunk but it's only a matter of one more drink before I am. I bop my head in rhythm to the song thumping through the speakers as I take a sip from my long island iced tea. I can't remember the last time I was able to get Terri and Clarissa to step inside of a nightclub let alone stay out past ten. From the sweat glistening on Clarissa's brow, I can tell they are having the time of their lives. The fellas are holding up the bar ordering back to back shots, scoping out women indiscreetly as not to be caught by their significant others. Elliott, the only one of us all that's "unattached", is off somewhere in the crowd chasing skirts. I don't know the name of this club. It's new and Grayson has said the name five times on the way here but I still can't remember.

"Farah Elise Acosta."

I freeze. Even over the loud music, I know that voice anywhere. I know I am alcohol induced but I can't mistake that voice. I turn to see Calvin Ethers grinning down at me. He hasn't changed; he's still handsome as ever.

"Damn girl, you look good."

Clarissa and Terri stop dancing behind me grilling him rudely. They know exactly who he is. He spots my sister, smiles. "Hey Clare!"

She frowns, yells out over the music, "My name is *Clarissa*. Hello Calvin." Her tone is icy. She is no more pleased to see him than I am.

He ignores her, looks back to me. "What are the odds of me seeing you here especially on your birthday. It is your birthday, right?"

I swallow hard and I suddenly feel sick to my stomach. "Yes," I stammer.

"Yeah, I thought so...Happy Birthday."

I drink down the rest of my liquor, I just want to get drunk enough not to remember this shit right here.

"Would you like to dance?" he asks holding his hand out toward me.

"I don't want to do shit with you Calvin," I spat.

He cringes at my words. "Farah, you're still mad at some shit from what....two years ago?! Give it a rest!"

"Fuck you!" My blood is boiling. He has just resurrected all of the dislike I have for him. I move to push past him but he grabs my arm roughly drawing me back.

"Get off of her," Terri yells.

I try to yank my arm away but his fingers dig deeper into my skin. "Let go of me!"

"Do we have a problem here?"

His tone is stern, his eyes blazing and I know he is trying hard not to flip shit. Grayson steps around just as he releases my arm. Raymond and Elliott are clean on his heels. This doesn't look like it's going to turn out well. Grayson towers over him by inches and suddenly, Calvin doesn't look so hard anymore.

"Nah," he mutters. "I was just wishing Farah a happy birthday."

Grayson's jaw clenches. I want to reach out and touch him, tell him to calm down but I know he is way past hearing that.

"And who are you?"

Calvin looks Grayson over, his lips curled up in a snarl. "Calvin."

"Ethers?"

Calvin looks over at me. I rub my arm where his grip once was, I'm sure there will be a bruise in the morning.

"Um...yeah. Who are you?"

"I'm her *boyfriend* and I really don't like what I just saw, man."

Calvin sucks his teeth, holds his hands up in surrender. "I have no problems, dude."

"Not the way I see it," Grayson says coldly, his hands open and close in a fist.

Elliott grabs his arm pulling him away. "Bro, he's not worth it. She's fine, lets go."

Tears burn my eyes. Even though I know it's not, I feel like all of this is my fault. I don't know whether to feel embarrassed or relieved that Grayson didn't knock his block off.

Clarissa puts her arms around me pulling me toward the exit. "Come on sis, we're leaving."

The ride back to Grayson's house is quiet, the kind of quiet that sits uncomfortably in the atmosphere. I'm sitting with my body facing him, admiring him. He is so tense, he hasn't looked my way since we left Terri's house.

I dare to speak, ask, "Did you mean what you said back at the club?"

Callously, he questions, "Mean what?"

His words hurt; I've never seen him this angry before.

"Why are you mad at me? I had no idea he was going to be there."

He sighs heavily massaging his temple. "I'm not mad at you, Farah. The thought of him with his hands on you...hurting you, it pisses me off. I'm just frustrated but it's not with you. I'm sorry."

His arm is resting on the middle console now. I reach out to hold his hand. He flinches at my touch but eases, complies as I slide my fingers through his.

"How is your arm?" he asks after a moment.

It's still a little sore but I lie and say, "It's fine."

"And yes Farah, I meant what I said back there. I want to be with you, I want you to be mine."

I smile as he raises my hand to his lips kissing the back of it.

"I'm sorry your night was ruined. I promise I will make it up to you."

"It's okay," I say softly. "I'm with you and that makes it the best birthday ever."

| Meet the Parents

"Yes, mami...he eats macaroni and cheese...woman, it's like one of his favorite foods...don't overdo it, you're meeting my boyfriend, it's not a wedding reception...Yes, he's very excited."

I look over at Grayson, he smirks at me.

"Oh gosh, I don't want papa to run him away...yes mami, we will be there on time...Ok, I need to go...We will see you at eight...love you too...bye."

It's Sunday afternoon. We're sitting in my living room. My laptop is resting on my thighs, my feet propped up in Grayson's lap while he watches a football game. It's been a month since we've made our relationship official, a month that has been building up to this very day: Grayson meeting my parents.

"Someone is excited," he teases. He is one to talk. He is just as anxious, if not more, as mami is. Meanwhile, I'm as nervous as a convict going before the parole board. I don't know what to expect.

I scuff. "More like ecstatic. She's been talking about this all week."

"I shall try to be on my best behavior."

I hit a few keys on the keyboard shutting the computer down. "Trust me baby, it's not you I'm worried about. Who the hell knows what will come out of their mouths."

"Well I'm ready. I've been waiting for you to introduce me to them. For a minute, I thought you might be ashamed of me."

I close the laptop and set it on the floor next to the couch. I can see him fully now. Though his tone seems playful, his expression is serious.

I cock my head to the side, puzzled. "Why would I be ashamed of you, Grayson?"

He shrugs. "Maybe I'm not good enough to meet your parents..."

"If you're good enough for me, you're good enough to meet them." *Oh hell, I sound like Terri.*

"So why has it taken this long for me to meet them?"

I sigh running a hand through my hair. "I don't want every man I engage myself with to meet my parents. That type of meeting is intimate, special. To be honest with you, I didn't want you to meet them until we were actually official."

"Why didn't you say something then?" He asks curtly.

"I didn't want to feel like I was begging."

"Begging?"

I huff, "Begging, pressuring you to commit to me. I didn't want to feel like that's what I was doing."

"How long would you have waited if I didn't commit when I did?"

I feel myself becoming annoyed.

How the fuck did this conversation happen?

"I don't know Grayson."

He grabs my ankles pulling me gently to his end of the couch, bridging the gap between us. "You are too good of a woman to settle. If I am not giving you what you want, I need you to tell me that. I would have been open to the conversation. I wanted the commitment just as much as you. I just didn't know how to go about saying it. We never talked about it so I assumed you might not be ready for all of that."

"So is it my fault that we didn't make it official sooner, because I didn't speak up?"

"I didn't say that."

"You're implying it."

He exhales loudly. "Let me retract the statement. I'm sorry. It's *both* of our faults for not being upfront with our feelings. We need to be more open with what we want and how we feel. I don't want to guess with you and I don't want you to guess with me. I want us to be on the same accord with things. I don't want you to feel like you can't come to me about something. I hope I've never made you feel that way."

I reach up running my fingers through his beard. "You haven't."

He leans in and kisses me softly. "I'm serious, Farah."

I pull him into me, my breasts pressed firmly against his chest. "I know."

It's the last days of summer and I seize the opportunity to put on the fitted, black sundress I bought on clearance at *Target* for dinner tonight. It's simple, casual, and sexy all at the same time. I watch him from the edge of my bed through the bathroom vanity mirror as he straightens his collar. I am thankful for my ability to talk him out of putting on a suit. His ass would have burst into flames the minute he stepped outside. Instead he settles for a Polo shirt, some slacks, and a pair of casual dress shoes. He is so nervous and I can tell by the way he tugs at the edge of his collar that just won't lay right.

"If you pull any harder, you're going to tear the collar right off. You look handsome, baby. Relax."

He gives me an edgy smile. "Thanks babe."

He sprays himself with cologne before vacating the bathroom.

"Are you sure I look okay?"

I scoot off the edge of the bed onto my feet, smooth a hand over my dress. I close off the space between us wrapping my arms around his waist. "I am positive, you look fine."

He presses his lips to my forehead. "Ok, lets go before my nerves get the best of me."

It's no surprise that my sister and Christian have beaten us here. I pull up behind Christian's black SUV and park. Inside, after using my key to gain access, the aroma of food is heavy in the air. My stomach grumbles. We decided against lunch earlier replacing it with sex and a two hour nap. Now I am starving and anxious to eat. Grayson looks around awestruck at the high vaulted ceilings in the hallway. I seize his hand pulling him in the direction of the den where I know the men are sure to be. Like the psychic I am, Papa and Christian are sitting on the couch leaning forward with their elbows on their knees waiting—waiting something to happen. And it does and they jump up like buffoons in a heap of cuss words.

"Gentleman, it's just a game!"

Papa's eyes light up at the sight of me. "Oh baby girl, look at you."

He hugs me close to him planting kisses on my forehead. "Every time I see you, you're glowing more and more."

I smile widely. "Well you can thank this guy. Papa, meet Grayson."

I step out of the way as papa reaches for Grayson's hand to shake. "It is good to *finally* meet you. My daughters speak highly of you. I'm Anthony Acosta."

"Grayson Powell, it's a pleasure to meet you sir."

Papa beams with much approval as if I have just introduced him to some celebrity or a hotshot businessman. "Well my wife is in the kitchen and she is dying to meet you. Go on in and introduce yourself and then come kick it with the men. Us men are not allowed in the kitchen for very long when the women folk are doing their thing."

That makes Grayson laugh and I can see his tension as it starts to fade. I link my arm through his leading him into the kitchen. Even with the many plates of food scattered about, pots and pans littering the stove, mami is graceful as she shuffles around the kitchen. Clarissa is sitting at the kitchen table flipping through a magazine.

"Good evening ladies."

"There you are!" Mami exclaims. "I was just asking Clarissa about you."

"We made it."

She hugs me tightly, nearly pushes me out of the way to get to Grayson. "And you are Mr. Grayson Powell, correct?"

Shyly, he says, "Yes ma'am, I am. It's nice to meet you."

She extends her arms out to hug him. I am thoroughly amused at the effort he has to put in to meet her halfway for the embrace. Mami is so damn short or Grayson is too damn tall.

"I'm so glad my daughter finally decided to bring you over to meet us."

"Me too," he says looking over at me, winks.

Clarissa looks up from her magazine long enough to say hello.

"Well look," mami says pushing him in the direction of the doorway. "We will talk a whole lot more in a little bit but for right now; you have to get your ass out of my kitchen. Go join the men in the den and I will have Farah bring you a beer or something, Cool?"

"Yes ma'am."

"Lord, he is handsome!"

Mami says once she is sure he is out of earshot.

I grin. "I told you he was."

"I mean, he really is Farah. I'm just glad to see you so happy baby."

"Me too," Clarissa agrees.

"Me three," I reply half serious and half jokingly.

Mami pulls the refrigerator open, grabs a beer, and shoves it into my hand.

"Don't just stand there; take your man a drink. And bring your ass right back so we can set this table."

And I do as I am told.

Mami is surely showing off tonight. Stuffed salmon over a bed of white rice, steak, sautéed asparagus, and green salad are on the menu. She even broke out the good china for this occasion. And despite her twenty questions about whether he likes macaroni and cheese, there isn't a noodle or a piece of cheese in sight.

"Everything looks amazing Mrs. Acosta," Grayson says after papa has finished saying grace.

"Thank you, honey. I hope it's as good as it looks."

"She's being modest, babe," I state. "She's really a chef."

"Is that right?"

She blushes. "Yes. I was a chef for a good number of years. That's how I met my husband actually. I catered one of his military dinners and it has been history ever since."

He smirks. "I see where Farah gets it from then."

Mami eats up his compliment giggling like a school girl.

"Anyway, I feel like I know so much about you already," Papa cuts in. "Farah talks about you often so I really just want to cut to the chase here. You know, see where you are looking to take things with my daughter. Marriage, if applicable...things like that."

Clarissa and I holler out in unison, "Papa!"

"What! We are all family in here."

I'm horrified, downright embarrassed but Grayson is laughing. He reaches over and squeezes my hand. "Babe, it's okay. I'm cool with talking about it."

"See baby girl, he is fine with it."

I get up retrieving a bottle of white wine from the bar mami always keeps stocked in the corner of the dining room. I can't take this sober.

Clarissa holds out her glass, "I think I'll need some of that."

Papa rolls his eyes. "My daughters are so dramatic. I'm serious though, Grayson. You and my daughter have been dealing with each other for about a year now and I'm quite curious as to where you see things going."

I down my glass in two full gulps immediately wishing I would have gone for the Bourbon instead. Whelp, it's too late now. I pour another glass to keep the party going.

Grayson takes a swig from his bottle of beer, clears his throat, replies, "To be honest with you sir, I haven't thought that far. I am just enjoying what we have right now. I don't want to rush anything. I have done that before and it did not end well. All great things take time to develop, you know."

Mami is staring at him like he's just given a presidential speech. I'm equally impressed by how well he has diverted the awkwardness of the conversation.

"I understand. That makes all the sense in the world. As a father of two daughters, I'm very overprotective and I'm sure you can understand that. I just want the best for them and I want them to be happy. Farah is the happiest I've seen her in a long time and I thank you for that. I just don't want to see her hurt again."

My eyes shift into my lap. I shuffle my fingers nervously. I cried over Calvin for weeks on end. It really frustrated papa, not to mention he was ready to kill his ass. I never want to be that way in front of my father again.

"I would never intentionally hurt Farah, sir. I really care about her...and...."

"Do you love her?"

A thick silence falls over the room, all eyes are on Grayson. Whole time, I just want to be swallowed up by the seat cushions. Clarissa and I reach for the bottle of wine at the same time. She seizes it first pouring another glass before handing it to me.

"Yes, Mr. Acosta, I *love* your daughter very much."

I don't catch the liquid before it spews from my lips; Clarissa erupts in a coughing fit.

"Farah Elise and Clarissa Jean get it together," Mami snaps.

Love? Did I hear that correctly? Just a few weeks ago, I had to find out he wanted to be with me during a heated altercation with my ex. Now I find out he loves me in front of my entire family.

You know, it would be really fucking great if I could find out before everyone else does!

A part of me is ticked off and the other part of me is overcome with emotions. Nonetheless, I feel on the verge of tears.

"Excuse me," I murmur abandoning my seat before I let my emotions show.

I'm in the half bathroom near the kitchen, gripping the sides of the sink so hard my knuckles are turning red. I wipe away fallen tears with the back of my hand. I can't even grasp why I'm crying but I am. The more I want them to stop, the harder they fall. There is a knock at the door. It is soft yet it startles me.

"Farah, open the door," Grayson says.

I grab a few tissues from the box sitting on the sink and try to dab at my cheeks without smearing what is left of my makeup. I study my face in the mirror. My eyes are bloodshot red and I have no way of hiding them.

"Farah!" This time his voice is sterner. "Open the door."

I unlock the door pulling it open for him to step inside. He pushes it closed behind him. I keep my head down looking at nothing in particular. I don't want him to see me like this. He presses his chest against my back wrapping his arms around me.

"Please tell me what is wrong. What did I do?"

My voice breaks as I speak. "I'm fine. You didn't do anything."

He supports my jaw in his hand forcing my head up, our eyes meet in the mirror.

"So why are you crying Farah? You lie so bad."

I wrestle myself free from his hold, turn to face him. The bathroom is barely big enough to contain us both.

"This is the second time you have failed to tell me something I need to know. Instead, I find out along with everyone else and then I am left feeling stupid. You love me? Were you serious or just saving face because my father asked you?"

He laughs, more out of frustration than anything else. "Was I just saving face? Seriously? I have no reason to lie to your father. I admit, I was dead ass wrong for not telling you first but to think I would lie about something like that...it's absurd!"

"Is it?" I snap

He scuffs. "You are so frustrating sometimes. My goodness, I have not been in love with anyone in a long time but I am with you..."

He pauses, takes a deep breath. "I really love you, Farah. That's it. It's not a lie or some façade I am trying to create to get in the good graces of your father."

And my eyes buckle again letting the tears flow.

"Stop crying," he murmurs wiping my tears away with his thumbs. "I don't like seeing you like this. I didn't think it was a big deal and obviously I was really wrong about that. Do you love me at all?"

"Yes," I tell him barely above a whisper. "I love you. I am so sorry for acting like this. I don't know what is wrong with me."

He pulls me into him. It is the most calming feeling to be in his arms. "You don't have to apologize. I was wrong. I am the one that needs to apologize. I'm sorry if I embarrassed you out there."

We stand in the clutches of silence for a few minutes. "I don't know if you are scared but I am," he utters. "It's been so long since I have committed myself to someone. It feels brand new to me now."

"It is really scary," I attest. "All of this, everything I feel about you."

He places a finger under my chin pulling it up so that my eyes meet his. "At least I'm not alone. We can be scared together. Together…I love the sound of that."

I Sad Goodbyes

My eyes struggle to open as if anchors are sitting atop them. My body feels heavy. I hear the pattering of rain on the window sill outside of Grayson's room and I realize why. I feel lazy, this is most Monday mornings but the rain isn't helping the cause. I'm awake twenty minutes before my alarm sounds. Grayson is snoring softly beside me. This man, *my* man...I love him. I snuggle up closer stealing his warmth. He moans sleepily wrapping his arm around me though his eyes never open. I drink in the smell of his body wash from his shower the night before. And now with fifteen minutes left to spare, I want to arouse him awake and let him fill me up until I have to get up for work. Just as I throw the sheets back from his waist, my cell phone blares with Boyz II Men's *Mama*. I scramble to answer it jolting Grayson awake. Mami never calls me this early and my thoughts immediately run away with me.

"Hello!" I answer. "Mami, is something wrong?"

"I'm sorry to disturb you honey," she says sullenly. "I just got off the phone with Audrey's husband. She passed away this morning."

The worst of my fears have settled but my heart aches at the thought of having lost Audrey.

"Oh mami," I cry. "He must be devastated."

"She was my good friend," mami sobs. "Even though she was sick, she fought so hard. I can't believe she is gone."

Anita Acosta is the strongest woman I know. Hearing my mother crying makes the reality clear that even the strongest people have their weakest moments. Grayson sits up beside me, stretches loudly.

"I know mami, I am so sorry."

"I'm going to go see Edward. I'll talk to you later baby."

She hangs up before I can say goodbye. Grayson puts a gentle hand to my back. My chest constricts before an outpour of tears consume me. He doesn't ask me any questions; he doesn't pry my emotions apart anymore than they already are. Instead, Grayson pulls me close to him letting me sob in his arms.

Audrey's funeral is the following Tuesday. Hundreds of people have come out to pay their respects. I had no idea how well known she was. I don't feel my best; in fact, I haven't for the past few days. Nonetheless, I put on the finest act of strength I can muster as her former intern and now owner of her business. I spot Erin in the crowd of people dressed morosely in black. She forces a smile in my direction and I to hers. I find my way to the front occupying a seat next to Mami, who is sitting next to Mr. Tine. Beside him is Stephanie, his daughter from a previous marriage. She is clutching his hand as he stares stone faced at his wife's casket. He loved that woman, stuck with her through any and everything. He is the epitome of what every man should be: a supporter, a lover, provider and a best friend. I peel my eyes away from him. The sight of him grieving is too much to bear.

After the ushers carry Audrey's casket out to the hearse and the mourners have spilled out into the street, I take the opportunity to go speak to Mr. Tine. When he sees me approaching, he gives me a weak smile. *Poor thing.*

"Thank you for coming Farah."

"Of course I would be here. I wouldn't dare miss it. I am very sorry about your loss."

I hug him to me. He seems fragile under my touch.

"It's okay; we knew this day was coming soon. She's not suffering anymore and that thought alone makes me feel a little better."

"If you need anything, anything at all, please call me Mr. Tine."

"Thank you."

I watch him walk down the carpeted aisle of the church, his daughter supporting his weight with her own.

"It was good seeing you Barbara, thanks for coming."

Mami envelopes the older woman in her arms, waves her off as she exits the church.

"Oh Farah, you look so weak baby," she tells me studying my face. "Go home and get some rest, okay."

I don't argue with her, standing on my own two feet is painful. I think I have some type of food poisoning or stomach virus. I haven't kept anything down in nearly two days, even water is a stretch. "Yes ma'am."

She pushes a few strands of hair away from my face. "Are you going *home* or are you going home?"

I chuckle lightly at her inquiry.

I answer, "I will be at the first home."

She smiles warmly cupping my face in her hands. "You are wasting money being in two different places."

"Oh mami," I say turning to leave. "You sound like your daughter."

"Well baby, she's not lying."

She is right on my heels following me out into the warming fall air. I retrieve my sunglasses from my purse; slide them over my eyes to block the domineering sunlight.

She gives me a stern motherly glare when I turn to face her. "You are barely home Farah. You pay rent just so the pictures on the wall have a place to hang. That makes no sense but whatever, it's your money."

This is coming from a woman that shops like clothes don't have price tags. I throw my arms around her, reply, "Look woman, I am going to go and do that thing you were talking about a few minutes ago. You know, rest. I will talk to him about it, okay?"

A hint of a smile crosses her mouth. "Thank you."

I shake my head with a laugh. "You and your damn daughter are a piece of work. You treat him like he's the best thing since running water."

"For you, he is."

She kisses me softly on the cheek, waits for me to get into the car.

The women in my family are something else, I think as I drive off

It's been three long days since Audrey's funeral and I am finally able to hold food down again. The doctor diagnosed me with a stomach virus prescribing me antibiotics to take twice a day for a week. I'm thankful to be recovering, I cannot bear to lose another pound after having lost ten already. I'm lying in bed underneath the weight of Grayson's arm watching a *Law & Order* marathon. He has been waiting on me hand and foot, working from home rather than keeping me out of his sight for those few hours. I turn to face him. It is a bit of a task considering my strength is not fully restored.

"Easy baby," he tells me as I shift, wincing from the pain in my lower back.

Once we are face-to-face, I ask, "What do you think about us moving in together?"

He looks at me with those big brown eyes, answers coolly, "I have thought about it."

That didn't answer my question, I say to myself sarcastically. "So? What are your thoughts?"

"What do you think I think about it?"

"For the love of Christmas Grayson Powell, answer the damn question!"

He laughs with amusement. "I think we should."

"Really?"

"No, for play play. Yes Farah…really."

I deserve that. "So I guess when my lease is up I can move in here."

"Or we can pay to break your lease now."

I frown. "Babe, I can just wait. That is a lot of money."

He shrugs. "No more than the money you have been wasting staying here damn near every night."

"My goodness, you sound like my freaking mother."

He replies, "She is a smart woman."

I can't help but laugh. He pulls me close to him and I let his soft breathing soothe me into sleep.

❙ Moving In

The next six months pass swiftly and before I know it, another spring is upon us. Despite Grayson's persistent nagging, I decide to wait the remainder of my lease out to move in. So in a few more days, he and I will officially be under one roof. *Ain't that nothing?!* The thought of *his* house becoming *our* house is unnerving. I don't know why. It's not like we haven't been doing it for the last year. Regardless, it is a big step and I am nervous as hell about it.

"Good morning, Ms. Acosta!"

It's a beautiful Friday morning, the warmest since the first day of spring. Erin is vibrant today, her smile on a thousand. She is like a breath of fresh air as soon as you walk though the door.

"Good morning, Erin. How are you?"

She replies, "Great, Ms. Acosta. I can't complain. Umm...can I ask you something?"

I stop in front of the receptionist area, rest my elbow on her desk. "Shoot."

"I'm doing this paper for class and I was *hoping* that I might be able to interview you for it."

My inner self gasps dramatically, a hand pressed to her chest. *Little ole me?*

"Um...sure, when would you like to do it?"

"Sometime next week if you can, it's not due until next month."

I smile warmly. "Absolutely, get with Cathy so she can set you up on my schedule. Lets get you this A, girl."

She claps giddily. "Thank you, Ms. Acosta."

"Erin, you've been working here for too long to keep calling me Ms. Acosta. Please call me Farah."

She blushes. "Ok...Farah."

"When did you buy all of this shit?"

Clarissa pulls a burgundy sweater off of its hanger, peers down at the price tag still dangling from the sleeve, and throws it to the side where it lands in the floor.

"What the hell do you think you're doing?"

"I'm taking it."

"Bitch what?" I sputter. "Put my shit back!"

"You weren't even thinking about it until you saw me with it. It still has the price tag on it. I guarantee you are not about to miss it."

"That's not even the point!"

"You're right because you don't have one."

My apartment is empty. The sounds of our voices bounce off the walls as we speak. All that is left are the clothes and shoes in my closet. After four years, I am finally moving out. The feeling is so alien, so bittersweet. Clarissa picks up a pair of heels and examines them.

"Oh no, bitch! Now I let you slide with the sweater but you can't have my Jessica Simpson's."

She frowns over at me tossing them into the plastic bin. "They are too high for me anyway," she snaps.

"I'm going to high a bump around your damn eye if you keep throwing my pumps like that."

She grins. "I love you too, Heffa. So where are you putting all of this stuff exactly?"

And that is the question of the week!

"We cleared out one side of his closet for my stuff but from the looks of it, that is not going to cut it."

"You think?" she mutters sarcastically. "How is my brother doing anyway?"

"If you have a brother, we all need to sit down and have a chat."

She laughs, says, "Bitch, you know what I mean."

I giggle. "He's doing well. He had a late business meeting so he couldn't be here to help."

"Are you really ready for this?" she asks seriously.

I pause readjusting my messy ponytail. "I think...I mean, yes. I'm still nervous."

"Oh honey, you better shake that off. You are three plastic bins and three...nope, four sheets full of clothes from being a resident of that house."

"I know, I know but I can't help it. It's such a big step, Clarissa. I just don't want to feel like I am making a mistake, you know. This type of leap can come back to slap me in my face."

"There goes Farah Acosta over thinking again. You leapt when you got into a relationship; you leapt when you told him you loved him, and what is one more leap of faith going to do? Don't forget that he loves you very much. I think that if he thought for one minute it couldn't work, he would have never agreed. Have faith in good things, trust me."

"You're right."

"I'm happy you have finally realized this."

I cut an eye at her. "Yeah whatever."

"Oh come on Farah," she exclaims holding up a pair of black suede pumps. "You still have the size sticker on the bottom!"

"I don't give a shit! Put my shoes down, the answer is no."

She sucks her teeth loudly tossing them into the plastic bin.

"Didn't you hear what I said about my damn shoes?"

I hop over a pile of clothes and lunge at her. She hollers playfully turning to flee but I catch her by the tail of her shirt. We fight like two kids in a tangle of laughter and love.

| Mother

I twitch, first my leg and then my whole body. My eyes pop open and I feel Grayson's large hands pressing my thighs apart. His tongue swirls around that part of me that swells stirring my sex drive awake. He is in his own world devouring me like he will never eat again. His mouth on me, his eyes on me, it's the most heightening feeling. I run my hand over his neatly cut hair, run my fingernails across the back of his neck. A groan escapes his throat and I feel the vibration against me. He stops, sits back on his heels. I'm left wanting and I'm ready to fuss him out for getting me all worked up.

"Over," he demands.

I quickly turn around onto my stomach. He grabs my waist roughly, pulls me up on my knees, and sinks down inside of me. The feeling is alluring, I'm heady. I press my breasts to the mattress arching my back gracefully. An orgasm sneaks up on me, rushes through my veins. He feels me tighten around him and his pace picks up in response. He wraps a hand around my long tresses, pulls my head back. I hear him grunt loudly and I know he is almost there. The sound of him enjoying me while I enjoy him triggers another ripple of pleasure. This time, it's forceful and my body convulses violently around him.

"Fuck!" he cusses loudly releasing himself inside of me. I collapse against the mattress, full body. I'm breathless; my legs are weak from the aftershock of my orgasm. He exhales loudly behind me. I feel the bed shift and then his lips on my shoulder.

"Good morning beautiful."

I bite my bottom lip with a smile. "Yes, it *is* a good morning. A girl can get used to this."

We are sitting on the edge of the whirlpool tub staring at the stick that rests on the bathroom sink. I look at Clarissa, she looks at me. I don't think a minute has gone by yet we have to wait for ten. She gnaws nervously on her fingernails; I reach out and swat her hand away.

"Don't do that," I snap.

She looks at me with nervous eyes. "Sorry, this is nerve racking."

Our eyes trail back over to the stick, we stare at it as though it's supposed to hop up and do a jig for us. I jump to my feet pacing aimlessly in front of her. I lean over wanting to peek.

"Don't peek," Clarissa yells at me!

I groan loudly, check the timer on my phone. It's only been five minutes, I'm losing my mind.

"What do you think he will say if it comes out positive?" Clarissa looks like she is about to shit a brick.

I sink down beside her. "I don't know, happy I think."

She smiles nervously. "That's good, I think so too."

After four of the longest minutes of my life, the timer buzzes. I scramble to my feet grabbing the stick between my fingers. I look down, swallow hard.

"Oh shit, what does it say?"

"It's...uh...positive."

She steps up next to me stealing it from my grip, wanting to see for herself.

"Shit!"

She grabs my shoulders looking me square in the face. "He'll be happy, right?"

Tears escape her eyes. I pull her to me in a tight hug. "Yes, he'll be happy. You're going to be a great mom."

I SECRETS

"Can I ask you something?"

I watch Grayson swallow his food before saying, "Yeah, go ahead."

It's a Friday night. We are in the living room eating Chinese food from the cartons while drinking beer and wine. He shifts his attention in my direction, waits for me to ask my question.

"Uh...how come you...um..."

He raises a curious eyebrow at me. "Spit it out, baby."

I take a deep breath, ask, "How come you don't talk to me about your parents?"

His face falls quickly. *Fuck!*

"They're dead," he says flatly.

I hadn't notice!

"I know that but you never speak on them, at all. You haven't even gone to visit their graves since I have known you."

"They're buried in Florida, that's not exactly around the corner."

I sigh. "Damn it Grayson, don't talk to me like I am stupid. Their birthdays have passed; anniversaries and holidays have all passed. Not once...*ever* once have you gone out there to visit them. You don't even speak about them, you or Elliott. I just want to know what's up with that."

He stirs pushing my legs from his lap, I have made him uncomfortable. My voice falls into a whisper as I say, "Never mind, lets just drop it."

"No, lets talk about it."

"Grayson..."

"Farah!" he snaps. "You brought it up so we're going to talk about it."

My stomach turns, my appetite is gone. I set my food down on the table, clench a throw pillow between my arms as if bracing myself for what he is about to say.

"They're not my real parents."

Nope, he didn't say that. He did. Yes, he did. He said it.

"Is Elliott not..."

He shakes his head. "No baby, he is my real brother. We were never separated when we got adopted."

My heart thumps through my ears. He has an awkward calmness about him like he has a heart made of coal.

"How old were you?"

"Three."

"And your real parents?"

He shrugs. "I don't know them and I don't care."

"How can you talk like that?" I demand.

'I have lost love for a lot of people, Farah. They are no different. They didn't want me; they never tried to find me. They gave me up so why should I go looking for them?"

A sob chokes me, steals my words. The coldest day of the year is no match against the look he gives me.

"Don't you do that! It's not your life to cry over."

He might as well have told me to do it. I hurry to wipe the tears that have fallen with the back of my hand. "It's hurtful to hear you say those things. I would think you owe the people that took you in some type of compassion. At least one visit out of the year."

He runs an exasperated hand over his face. "This is why I don't like talking about my past," he utters in a softer tone.

He takes a long pause and I feel like the grim reaper of silence is about to come take us away. Finally, he says, "I have flowers delivered to their gravesites on their birthdays and some holidays. I haven't been back to Florida in years and I haven't been to visit them since we put them in the ground. I know it sounds heartless, Farah and I am sorry for that. I have gone through so much over these past few years and I have learned to detach my feelings along the way. I thought Elliott was going to have a heart attack when I told him I loved you. I haven't loved anyone in years. I told myself I would stop being such an angry person and open up to someone or at least try. Then you happened and here we are."

"What else have you been through?"

He shakes his head with a laugh but it's not an amused laugh rather one of dismay. "Lets not go there, please. I don't like talking about my past. I just said that."

I have that sinking feeling in the pit of my stomach. I think it's best we stop talking about it anyway.

"Fine, I'll let it go."

"It's so much Farah and I...I don't want to keep secrets away from you but I just need to prepare myself for that conversation first."

I put a hand up to silence him. "It's fine."

He grabs my wrist gently pulling me close to him. "Farah, it's not fine."

"I love you Grayson and if it hurts you that much, I will wait until you are ready to talk about it."

"I'm sorry." The anger I once harbored dissipates at the sound of his voice. There is so much regret, so much hurt and it is more than I can withstand.

I reach out and stroke his face. He kisses my palm lightly. "It's okay," I tell him. "We can talk about it when you are ready."

His eyes are dark and pained but his kiss is full of passion. "I love you, Farah. Thank you."

"What do you think about this?" I point at some name brand watch through the glass case.

Elliott frowns. "It's okay."

"It's the fourth one we've looked at; I have to choose something to get him for his birthday."

"Actually you don't. Grayson hasn't had a real gift for his birthday since he was a kid. If he wants material things, he will pay for it with his own dough. Really Farah, you don't have to get him anything."

I tap a finger against his bicep. "Is there a heart? Is there a heart in the house tonight?" I sing playfully.

He laughs loudly.

"I mean humor me, Elliott. Would there be anything he wants?"

He drums a finger against his chin in thought. "Besides you, there's nothing I can think of."

"Geez Louise!"

I peek over at a case of rings; cringe when I see the price tag on one of them. "This shit is overpriced anyway, lets go."

"He can't stop talking about this trip to Dominican Republic; I don't think you can beat that."

I spent half a year secretly planning a romantic getaway for Grayson and me to the Dominican Republic. I strategically set it for the weekend of his birthday and gave him the tickets in a gift box as an early present. It's true. The trip is all he talks about but yet and still, I feel like I should be getting him something else. Too bad, his brother is no help at all. We spill out into the mall and I lead us toward *Macy's*.

"He told me you two were adopted," I blurt out.

Elliott's eyes widen a little but his tone is steady. "Yes, that's correct."

"Something bad happened to him, didn't it?"

He grabs my arm, pulls me down onto one of the benches. "Nothing bad happened to him, Farah. Don't over think things. Grayson just has a big heart and he's let a lot of people step all over it. He's been in some fucked up situations but other than being adopted and losing our foster parents, he's maintained a pretty average life. I'm taking it that he hasn't gone into details with you."

Every night that I sleep next to him, I think of what ill secrets may be lurking in his past. He is so guarded and it bothers me. To think that there is a place within him that I cannot reach, it's hurtful.

"No, he won't."

"That's Grayson for you. Give him time, he'll come around. Look Farah, my brother is one of the most standup gentlemen I've ever met and I'm not just saying that because we're related. His past is rocky but everybody has something hidden in their closet of skeletons that they just prefer not to talk about. He'll open up to you every way possible but his past, his past is a slow process to get through. He's not an axe murderer or an ex-felon. He's just Grayson Powell and he's been hurt a time or two."

"Are you sure I don't need to keep a gat under the pillow?"

Elliott erupts with laughter. "No Farah, you can keep the gun in the drawer."

| Oceans and Airplanes

I have never seen a sight more breathtaking than the one I do now. I can't even complain about the thirty minute drive from the airport to the hotel, the scenery is exquisite. Beautiful, piercing blue waters and white sandy beaches surround *Hotel Bávaro*. The manicured lawn is the brightest green I have ever laid eyes on, lined with exotic plants and palm trees. The driver of the airport shuttle that has transported us to this lap of luxury helps us unload our baggage onto the luggage cart for easy transfer into the lobby. The front desk clerk is stunning. She has immaculate tanned skin, long dark hair with not a strand out of place, and eyes the color of the ocean waters. I don't even want to know how great her body must look underneath her uniform. I am immediately jealous.

Her accent is as thick as papa's. She says, "Welcome to Dominican Republic's *Hotel Bávaro.*"

"Hello, I'm checking in under Farah Acosta."

When I look over at Grayson, he is eyeing her every move. I roll my eyes settling my attention back on her as she types something into the computer.

"Yes, Ms. Acosta. Let me get your keys." She disappears into the back office.

"Are you done gawking? Can she have her face back now?"

He laughs with embarrassment. "Am I sensing jealousy, Ms. Acosta?"

His hand runs down the length of me, squeezes my backside. "Jealous? Of her? She's only sickeningly beautiful and you've been staring her down since we walked up here. Why would I be jealous?"

He chuckles. "Ok, you've made your point. I love you though."

I roll my eyes. "Say anything to save your ass from experiencing a night on the hotel couch."

"Is it working?"

I giggle. "No, Mr. Powell, it's not working."

Damn, I hear him say playfully under his breath as the beauty comes back with our keys.

We are taken to a private villa a few feet away from the front lobby. It's so exclusive; you get actual brass keys instead of the card ones. Inside, the hallway is rather compact with a single door giving way to the laundry room. Further in is a fully equipped kitchen that overlooks the small dining room. A bottle of champagne sits on the counter with a card welcoming us to the resort. Compared to the other two rooms, the living room is massive. There is a patio door that leads out to a private swimming pool and Jacuzzi. Upstairs is a master bedroom with a connecting bath. It reminds me of our own with the tub separated from the shower, duel showerheads, and his and her sinks. There's a large window overlooking the entire resort, giving view to the ocean and personal beach that sits behind it. Overall, it's cozy and perfect for our romantic weekend. The bellman sets down our bags, takes the generous tip from Grayson, and goes about his way.

"You really didn't have to bring me here," he says easing up behind me as I stand looking out at the pool. "I would have been perfectly fine celebrating my birthday at home."

"I'm being selfish. I want you away from everyone, with me and only me. I guess it's kind of like a gift to me too."

I turn to face him, he smirks. "All we had to do was close the blinds, lock the doors, and turn off our phones."

I reach down and unbuckle his shorts, my eyes never leaving his. "And risk the chance of someone dropping by. That would be foolish of me..."

I push his shorts and boxers down at once around his ankles, take his growing member in my hand. He sucks air in through his teeth rolling his head back. Watching him come apart in front of me, feeling him grow in my palm turns me on to the highest degree. I sink down to my knees taking him into my mouth. He gasps above me and I'm instantly wet. I take him in more, more until I can't take another inch. He eases his fingers into my hair gripping a handful, tugging gently. I use two hands to hold him both working simultaneously as I ease my mouth up and down his shaft.

"Shit!"

I find a rhythm and move. Spit seeps from the corners of my mouth, sloppy head.

"Okay Farah, geez...I'm about to come," he begs.

His body stills, grip tightens in my hair. He comes like a runaway train, his goodness discharging to the back of my throat. I stand back to my feet wiping my mouth with satisfaction.

"I'm going to put my bathing suit on," I tell him turning on my heels.

And I leave him there, undone and breathless.

"I think we should stay here forever."

Grayson looks out over the tops of the trees at the sky smeared with colors of burnt orange and yellow. The sunset is beautiful, romantic. After delicious sex in the shower, we order dinner from the hotel's restaurant and have it delivered to the villa. Ice clinks loudly around in his glass as he sips the brown liquid, white Hennessey from the hotel's store.

"And do what?" I ask sipping from my glass of wine. I watch him from across the patio table, lost in a state of solitude.

"Have a lot of sex, get married, have kids..."

"All of that with *me*?"

"We have a lot of sex already..."

I cut my eyes in his direction. "I'm talking about the marriage and kids," I specify.

He grows silent. "It's just a thought."

"A very ambitious thought," I murmur.

"I can't believe in a couple of months, it's going to be two years that we've been together. Time is racing."

Way to change the subject. I decide against pointing out his attempt at shifting the conversation. Instead, I say, "It is."

"Do you believe in this...in us?"

I'm perplexed; the question throws me off guard. "Run that back..."

He takes another drink from his glass. "Nothing."

"That's a crazy question, Grayson. Of course I do, don't you?"

"I thought you didn't hear me," he says, sarcasm lacing his voice.

I roll my eyes. His own are still fixed on the darkness that is beginning to settle over us.

"It's a little insulting, don't you think? Are you saying you don't believe in us?"

He shrugs. I sit up in my chair; take few deep breaths to keep from flying off the handle.

"I don't speak shrug," I snap.

"I love you Farah but I've loved before and it all fell apart. I have a hard time believing that this could be different."

"That's really not some shit to say to the woman you love that brought you all this way for your birthday. When have I ever given you the impression that this would not last?"

"You haven't but neither did...never mind. Forget I asked."

I am fuming and the wine pumping through my system isn't helping me much. I slam the glass down on the table, lucky it didn't shatter in my palm. "You're kidding me, right? You come out of your face and basically tell me you think nothing of our relationship and I am supposed to just dismiss it like it's nothing serious. Fuck you Grayson and fuck every woman that has ever done you wrong. I am not them and never will be them. If I wanted to hurt you, I damn sure wouldn't spend my hard earned coins on this trip. I would never hurt you; it's the furthest thought from my mind."

I am so angry, beyond it. Tears of frustration begin to build, threatening to release.

"So prove it."

I sputter, "Prove what?"

"Prove to me that you will never hurt me."

"What the fuck do you think I've been doing for the past two years? Twiddling my damn thumbs? I think you've had too much to drink, you're acting crazy."

I stumble to my feet barreling for the door. He is right on my heels. He grabs my arm spinning me around. "Marry me Farah."

And I laugh, right in his face. I laugh like he's just told me a hella funny joke.

"I think your damn Hennessey is defected," I say curtly. "You should take that shit back."

His face is stone. He is dead ass serious. "Please."

I snatch my arm from his grip. "No."

My words wound him and I can tell by the pain pillowing in his eyes. It makes my heart cry out and I realize how cowardly I am against my feelings for him.

"Why?"

"Who hurt you? Who is she?"

He blinks repeatedly. "That's not answering my question."

"I don't care, answer mine."

"No."

I turn to head upstairs, say over my shoulder, "Then I'm not marrying you."

He takes the steps two at a time behind me. His presence is dominating, close like a second skin.

"We have gone over this. I don't like talking about my past. You said when I'm ready."

"Oops! I lied! You just asked me to marry you not even two minutes ago and you think I am supposed to say yes. Hell to the no! I love you, God knows I do but I refuse to marry someone that cannot be open with me. You said so yourself, it was *you* that said we need to be more open. I suggest you find something deep down inside of you and start coughing up some facts! Talk to me or I will *never* marry you. I mean it."

Oh. Is that right? I shock myself with my own words.

I don't realize I'm crying until a tear hits my collarbone. I can't register his emotions, his expression is blank.

"Everything?" he asks.

My voice is broken, shaking under my words. "Everything, I want to know it all."

He sighs loudly. "Okay."

I MEMORY LANE

We are sitting in the middle of the king size bed, our eyes fixed on each other.

"I was three when we were adopted, Elliott was nine. Mr. and Mrs. Powell were a military family. Mrs. Powell couldn't have any kids though. They treated Elliott and I well, we never needed for anything. I grew to love them very much especially mom, she and I were the closest. The weekend that they died, there was a military banquet going on in New York. My father was being honored there for something, I can't remember. Anyway, my mother really didn't want to go because the weather was calling for snow. Somehow my father convinced her and they flew out from Florida on a Friday night. I know some of this you have heard before but I am just recapping..."

"Grayson...baby, I'm listening. I don't care how many times I've heard it, I'll listen *every* time."

He forces a smile. "Okay. So Saturday night when they were leaving the banquet, a truck hit a patch of ice and rammed into their rental car head on. I was at my Godmother's house when we got the news. I was devastated and I think that is putting it mildly. They never kept the fact that they were not our real parents away from us. When they died, I just lost it. I had lost every parent I ever had as if I was cursed or something. Elliott was away at school and he flew back immediately to be with me. Our Aunt Shelby came down from Ohio to help with the funeral arrangements. I don't think she ever liked us. I never told you this Farah but my adopted mother was white, my dad was black. I just think it never sat well with Aunt Shelby that her sister not only had a black husband but two black children too. She never really approved of their marriage either from what I gather. She came around seldom through the years. A real bitch, I tell you."

"Grayson!"

"I'm being honest with you. She stayed for a few weeks after the funeral. I hated every minute of it. She funded the funeral and didn't hesitate to make it known that she did. After we settled all of their accounts, life insurance, stocks, and sold the house, we paid that bitch back and move to Alexandria. We moved into a small, two bedroom apartment. I enrolled in the nearest high school and Elliott went back to finish his degree at Howard University. The whole ordeal of losing my parents fucked me up. Eventually, I opened back up and became just a normal happy, go lucky teenager again."

I am hanging on his every word. I feel as if I am about to fall off of a cliff when he pauses to clear his throat.

"Then I went to college and started meeting women, having sex, and getting into relationships. I have to admit, I was pretty vulnerable. I got into relationships with so many women and each and every time I thrust my entire being into them. I got hurt every time...*every* time. So I went through this phase of just fucking and running. I slept with woman after woman never giving them a chance to latch on, never giving me a chance to feel anything for them. I ducked and dodged feelings like a bullet. I was tired of being hurt so I didn't give a fuck about women and how they felt. Then I met Tracy...Tracy Peters. She changed my whole point of view. Farah, I loved that woman about as much as I loved myself."

The thought of him loving another woman especially to that extent is uncomfortable. I stir with uneasiness in front of him.

Noticing my standoffishness, he says, "I'm sorry, you probably didn't want to hear that. She really helped me though. She was forceful and she wouldn't just let me run out of her life as easily as the other women had. It was like I had been doing it for so long, I forgot what I was even running from. So I stopped and I committed to her. It was two of the best years of my life until I found out she had gotten pregnant...and it wasn't mine."

My eyes enlarge. His demeanor changes, he's delving in that very place that has destroyed his trust.

"We were living together at the time. She was taking a nap in the bedroom but she had left her phone in the living room. I noticed her doctor's office was calling so I answered it. It was an automated system telling her that her test results had come in. I know that doesn't seem out of the ordinary and it didn't to me either...at first. Then it dawned on me that not even three months before, she was telling me about how she was going to the doctor for her annual exam or whatever the fuck you women do every year. Now I know it doesn't take three months to come back with some test results so I asked her about it. That's how I found out she was pregnant..."

My mouth is dry. I try hard to swallow against the lump forming in my throat.

"She was two months pregnant. She told me she thought to lie about it but couldn't bear to hurt me anymore. She had cheated on me. The one woman I chose to open up to, let into my life had cheated on me destroying my faith in women all over again. The worst part of it all wasn't that she was pregnant. No, the worst part was that she was pregnant by Elliott."

He could have slapped me and the blow would have been softer than the one I received from his words.

"Wait, are you talking about your brother Elliott?"

Sullenly, he shakes his head. "Yes, she never did tell me how it came about but it happened and more than once. The woman that slept next to me every night was *fucking* my brother. Him and his wife separated after she found out and then filed for divorce a year later. It took me two years to start speaking to Elliott again. It wasn't too long before I met you that we had settled our differences."

I am speechless. The man I consider a brother to me, the man that was just helping me pick out gifts for Grayson is a fraud. He's a cause for why Grayson is the way he is. How can he act so unaffected knowing eventually I will find out? What kind of brother, the only *real* family he has, would do something like that to him? My head is spinning with questions. I feel bamboozled. I wipe an invading tear away.

"And the baby?"

"I wanted her to keep it. It's not the child's fault for their actions. I didn't want her having an abortion off the strength of me. So she kept it and she and her son live in Delaware now. She comes to visit on holidays and most times she's here, Elliott is nowhere to be found. That's how I know; he rarely mentions her name to me. It's not that I can't love; it's just that I'm fearful of what will happen once I allow myself to love. I want to believe that what we have will be the best thing to ever happen to me. The truth is, I don't...not fully at least. Your love is something completely different from what I felt with Tracy. It's overpowering. Even when I was trying my best not to fall for you, I fell harder. It wasn't like that with her. A man cannot help but to be drawn to you, Farah. Loving you is as easy as breathing. I know that sounds really cliché but it is and this is coming from a broken man."

My inner woman drags her step stool out, climbs on top of it, and folds her arms in victory.

Thank you bitches, the queen is here.

No matter how I feel on the inside, it doesn't overshadow the matter at hand. The elephant is still in the room.

My voice is low, nearly mute. "And you think all of those pinned up insecurities are going to mysteriously disappear by getting married."

"I want to be with you so yes."

I shake my head as though what I'm hearing is muffled and I'm trying to clear my ears. "You make no sense Grayson Powell. It's one thing to want to be with me but it's another thing to want to spend the rest of your life with me. You think I want to marry a man who has no confidence in what we have? How fair is it to me that I give my all, every part of me and you give me whatever you want me to have of you. That's bullshit and I won't...I will *not* marry you under those pretenses. I know what happened between Tracy and your brother did a number on you but you will not hold her fuck up over *my* head! You *will* give me what I have rightfully worked for: your heart, *all* of you! Not just a little bit but the whole kit and caboodle. I want you to trust me, believe in me, and believe in us..."

My tears begin to break me down, stealing my voice away from me. Grayson pulls me into his lap cradling me against his chest.

"Shh, okay Farah. I'm sorry, I'm sorry babe. I want to give you that, I swear I do."

"No," I stammer pulling away from him. "Don't make me an empty promise, do it. You don't want to marry me, Grayson. You just love the thought of having me for as long as you can hold me. Deep down you are anticipating the moment that I hurt you just so you can continue to convince yourself that being hurt is normal. You can hold on to the hurt that someone else inflicted on you or you can hold on to me, the woman you want to be your wife. I will not play second best to your past. Not when I am taking you just as you are with all of your fucked up shit in tow."

"I will trust you. I will love you. I will give myself to you completely. A part of me was scared that you would go running for the hills if I told you about how fucked up my past is, my family is. This very moment right here makes it clear that I want you in my life forever. I do want you to marry me and not just because I love the thought of it but because I really want it."

"No Grayson, that's what you are good at...running. You should be a track star by now."

"I deserve that. I am really sorry I couldn't bring myself to tell you this sooner. It's really hard, Farah. At least, if nothing else, understand that."

"I do. It's just...it's a lot to take in. You don't realize how much it hurts me to be with a man that is so guarded. Now that I know why, it hurts even more to know that she has ruined my ability to have all of you."

"I'm sorry..."

"I don't need you to apologize, Grayson. You can keep those, please."

"I want you, the thought of you and everything in between. I want it all...forever."

When any woman would be elated by his words, my heart sinks. My inner woman is fussing with me to say yes, rooting me on with a set of pom-poms. I can't bring myself to do it.

"No."

My words catapult him into another world. I clasp my hand around his jaw, forcing him to stay tuned into me. "My answer isn't no indefinitely, okay. I hear you, I hear every word but behind those words is a man that is still unconvinced. We need time, *you* need time. You have not fully healed. I can see it in your eyes, Grayson Powell. You're not ready. I need and I want all of you and you cannot give me that just yet."

As if stuck behind some invisible barrier, I see the tears in his eyes that will not fall.

"Okay," he mutters freeing himself from my touch.

He says nothing else to me. He just turns and walks out of the room. Now I am all alone with my thoughts and my ragged emotions. I cry. I cry until my heart can't bear it any longer, until my soul is aching under the weight of my sorrow. I let my tears take me under; drown me until sleep throws me a raft.

⏐ The Morning After

My eyes ache, my head is rocking at the temples. The curtains are closed tightly blocking any form of sunlight from coming through. I'm surrounded by darkness, alone. I stagger from the bed into the bathroom. I stare at myself in the mirror. My eyes are swollen from crying the night before. I look like yesterday, a fucking mess. I brush my teeth; press a hot rag to my eyes a few times to bring down the swelling. I peel my body out of the dark blue sundress I fell asleep in, wash the important parts, and redress in a t-shirt and shorts. I take the tangled mess I call hair and push it back into a ponytail and retreat downstairs to find Grayson. Through the drawn blinds, I see him sitting outside on the patio. I grab my shades off of the dining table and step out into the warmth of a new day.

"Good morning," I say half expecting him to respond.

"Morning," he says flatly.

I eye the glass of Hennessey in his hand. "It's a little early to be drinking, don't you think?"

He raises the glass to his lips and takes a sip. "Nope, it's twelve o'clock somewhere."

"Are you mad at me?" I can't help but ask though I already know the answer by his body language.

"Why would I be upset?"

"You know why."

"We're good, Farah. Everything is fine."

Frustrated, I grab the glass from his hand and plant it on the table. I straddle my legs on either side of him giving him nowhere else to look but at me. And although my eyes can barely withstand the struggle against the sunlight, I snatch the sunglasses off my face and toss them on the table.

"We're not going to do this today. We are on vacation, we're supposed to be happy and having fun. Please tell me if you are mad at me for…for not saying yes…to marrying you."

He cradles my face in his palms pulling me close as he plants soft kisses on my eyelids, down to my lips in a kiss.

"I'm sorry," he whispers. "I know you don't want to keep hearing that but I really am."

"Are you upset?"

"I was. I'm more frustrated than anything mostly with myself. I understand your position."

I run my fingers through his beard. "Do you really or are you just saying that because I look like shit."

"…no thanks to me."

"Answer my question."

He runs his hands down the sides of my face, my collarbone, and across my erect nipples poking through the fabric of my t-shirt. They continue their journey, resting finally on my backside.

"No, I really understand. Maybe I'm not as ready as I think I am. Maybe we really do need a little more time. I really don't want to lose you, Farah. That's the truth of the matter. The thought alone is devastating to me."

"You won't."

"Okay."

"Do you believe me?"

He alters his weight so that he can sit more comfortably and I feel him throbbing against me. Even in this moment of confusion and utterly unrefined emotion, I crave him.

"Farah, I said okay."

"And I asked you if you believe me. Answer me."

He scuffs in shock at my abrasiveness. "I believe you Farah Elise..."

He pauses. He closes his eyes tightly, inhales sharply. "I trust that I won't lose you to all of my nonsense."

"Let me be the judge of what is nonsense. What you have been through is nothing close to that."

"If you say so, I beg to differ. Any other woman wouldn't be so understanding, so patient. Thank you. I love you."

He grabs the back of my neck forcefully pulling me into a kiss full of immense passion. He grabs the edging of my shirt lifting it up and over my head. His large, overbearing hands cover my breasts like baseball mitts. My nipples dance playfully against his palm. In one move, his warm mouth is wrapped around one sucking gently. I moan loudly from the electrifying sensation racing through me. I move against him, the friction from his trapped erection drives my insides wild.

"I love you too," I pant as his mouth covers the other breast. He pinches my nipple gently between his teeth and I practically spill over in his lap. "I want you...in the bed...make love to me."

My legs wrapped firmly around his waist, he lifts me and carries me upstairs. And in the most agonizingly slow, rousingly passionate way, he makes love to me like he never has before.

| FORCED BEHAVIORS

After four glorious days in the Dominican Republic, we are back in reality's grasp. I am exhausted. I got next to no sleep due to a hollering baby on board. Above all of that, I know within the next few minutes I will have to face Elliott. That thought in itself is draining. I don't know how to act around him anymore. It has been years since it all happened but the wound Grayson bears from their actions is still fresh. Deep down, I want to march outside and tell Elliott which part of the depths of hell he can go to and how to get there. I can't and I won't but only because of Grayson... *only* because of him.

"Farah...Farah! Snap out of it."

Grayson nudges me shoving the handle of my suitcase into my hand.

"Sorry," I mutter.

He eyes me cautiously. "What's the matter with you?"

I tilt the bag on its wheels and make my way toward the exit. "I know you heard me, Farah. Don't play with me."

He jogs a little to catch up to me, grabs my arm rearing me backwards. "Woman, what is the problem and don't tell me nothing."

"I just want to go home, Grayson."

He frowns. "I see what this is about. Farah, I am begging you. Don't act strange towards my brother. Not now, okay."

I stare at him; grill him like I want to cook his ass for breakfast, lunch and dinner.

"Sure," I say through clenched teeth before turning to walk away.

Outside, a blanket of humidity falls over me. It's not as hot as it was in the Dominican Republic but it's hot enough. Elliott is leant against his car smiling brightly as we walk up.

"Welcome back!"

He and Grayson exchange hugs.

"You're lucky I came back," Grayson jokes.

I push my mouth up into a smile as he reaches for a hug. "Hey sis."

"Hey," I say dryly.

He frowns at my half attempt at a hug. "You okay?"

Grayson's eyes fly in my direction.

I say hastily," I'm fine, just tired. It was a long flight."

"I understand. Let me help you with your bags. We need to get out of here before rush hour traffic. You know how Mondays can be."

I sink into the backseat drawing my attention to the streets of DC as they fly by outside of the window. Even with the air conditioning blaring from the vents, I feel hot underneath Grayson's scolding glare.

"Get out!"

Clarissa's mouth hangs open as I finish dishing the finale of everything that happened on my so-called romantic getaway.

"The finest men always have some shit with them."

"Luckily, you never had to deal with anything."

She nods in agreement, pauses for a second in thought, and exclaims, "Forget you bitch, my man is fine."

I bellow with laughter. "But seriously, I love that man so much and everything in me wanted to say yes but my mind said no."

"They have some real fucked up *Lifetime* movie shit going on. I think you made the right decision honestly. Time heals all wounds. What's going to happen when you finally say yes? Wait...is you going to say yes?"

I chuckle both out of hilarity and frustration. "At this point, I can't call it. I feel like I am going to explode if I don't say something to Elliott. You know how I am Clarissa, I can't just let things linger."

"Okay, bump all of that. Are you going to marry this man or not?"

I stare at her through bemused grey eyes. That's the part I hadn't thought about, the part I've desperately tried to avoid.

"I meant what I said. Grayson is still so much hidden and there are no *secrets* about that. I can't marry a man like that. I would be torturing myself and lying to him all at the same time. Not now. Somewhere down the line, if there is a somewhere, I might."

She pouts over at me. "I really like him, Farah. He is so perfect for you."

"I love him, Clarissa but it's just not our time."

I shift nervously in my seat feeling like a loner for sitting all alone. There is no one paying me any mind. In fact, everyone around me is by themselves. Some on their computers, others indulging in a book or newspaper, and the remaining stare aimlessly out of the window at the lunch crowd as they pass by. I am part of the remainder pretending to find something interesting out the window to avoid the awkward moments of eye contact with other patrons. The door of *Starbucks* flies open and Elliott comes bustling in wearing a crisp white dress shirt, black slacks, and a blue and white bowtie. He spots me, smiles, and hustles through the waiting customers over to the table.

"By now, I shouldn't be surprised at how much people around here can't drive," he huffs hugging me quickly before occupying the seat adjacent to me.

I smile forcefully. "Yeah, I'm not sure why you are still surprised either."

"So what's up?"

He doesn't even try to ease into the conversation. No small talk. No asking me how my Wednesday is going or nothing, just right on into it.

"I wanted to talk to you about something," I tell him. I am suddenly losing all nerve to say what needs to be said.

His eyebrows furrow. "And that would be."

Hold your horses, I'm coming.

I take a deep breath, stop thinking, and just spit it out. "Grayson told me what happened. You know, in his past."

He sits back against his chair, his face blank as a fresh sheet of paper. "And you choose here, now, of all times and places to want to discuss this?"

Snappy? Ok, I see how this is going to go.

"I thought a public place would be fitting so I can't cuss you out the way I want to."

He crosses his arms over his chest, emotionless. "And why would you do that. You have no reason to be mad."

My eyes widen in shock. I have to take a moment to compose myself before I open my mouth again. "Your brother proposed to me Elliott and I told him no. Would you like to know why?"

His whole script flips, face softens. "Why did you do that to him Farah?"

"If I marry him, I am only kicking dirt over what is still there. I can't do that. He can't even sit in the same room as her. He hides from her like some escaped convict. I bet he hasn't even met your child, huh?"

"He hasn't," he says softly. "I have tried but he won't do it."

"See. That's not healthy, Elliott. I don't care how many pieces you want to slice it into. All of those things affect us. Everything we have built will falter under the weight of his past. He doesn't fully believe in us and that is the most hurtful thing he has ever said to me. If he can forgive you then he can at least forgive her for the sake of his nephew."

He sighs. "It sounds all well and good but he won't ever do that. He hates that woman and hate is a strong word. He flips if I ever mention her name. For a moment, I thought she had ripped out his heart and ran away with it until you came along."

"Yeah, well I'm not marrying your brother..."

"Farah, please..."

"There is no debate about it, Elliott. Would you marry a woman that still buckles under the name of her ex-boyfriend? Would you be able to fully love a woman whose ex still holds *that* much power over her?"

He shakes his head no.

"I thought so."

I stand to my feet gathering my purse and iced coffee from the table. "I know I am probably going to get my ass handed to me once he finds out I spoke with you about this but I couldn't hold it in any longer."

The blank stare is back but this time his eyes hold so much sorrow in them.

"Oh and Elliott, to be technical, ripping out his heart was a joint effort. Enjoy the rest of your day."

| CHANCE ENCOUNTERS

"First of all, I'm really unhappy with your mother sending us on a wild goose chase for some damn cranberry sauce"

It is Christmas Eve. Clarissa and I are walking the aisles of *Wal-Mart*, the fifth store we've been to in an hour in search of cranberry sauce per mami's request. I am irritated, I want to get back to my warm house, drink spiked egg nog, and sneak off to fuck my man while everybody else is in the kitchen cooking. But no, I'm in crowded ass Wally world with my pregnant sister searching for some shit that I don't even eat.

"Man, tell me about it! It is cold as shit outside too, this better be the fanciest can of cranberry sauce in the history of everdom."

I laugh but my laughter quickly turns into irritation at the sight of a full display of cans.

"Oh here goes some," Clarissa says gingerly.

We should have come here in the first fucking place.

"No, that's not just *some.* That's four stores worth of cranberry sauce. I don't even know why I listened to your mother to begin with; we could have just come here and saved my gas money."

Clarissa tosses four into the basket and I nearly mow down an old lady trying to get to the cash register. I flip open the pages of a tabloid, peruse the lies and over embellished stories that fill it as we wait in line to ring up our items.

"Farah, he's so adorable."

Clarissa coos at the little boy sitting in the cart in front of us. The sight of him makes my ovaries ache. He has enormous brown eyes, a bright smile, and a contagious laugh. Clarissa waves at him playfully and he erupts into a fit of giggles. He is the cutest thing. The woman pushing the cart turns around briefly to see what he is laughing at. I assume she must be his mother. Her eyes meet ours; she smiles warmly before turning back around.

"You like the pretty women, Jaime?" she asks him.

He laughs wildly at her question.

"He is staring at you, Farah. You know what they say about that?"

I narrow my eyes at her. "No, what do they say?"

She reaches out running a hand across my stomach. "It means you're next."

I slap her hand away. "Oh no you don't...trying to jinx me!"

"Hey, don't shoot the messenger. I'm just telling you what the saying is."

When I look back at the little boy, it is as if looking into the eyes of someone I know. I feel like I have seen him before and in DC that could very well be possible.

"I can't wait until this little boy gets here, I'm anxious."

"Well you better un-anxious yourself; you have a ways to go."

Clarissa frowns. "Yeah, whatever."

Twenty minutes and a price check later, we finally make it up to the front to pay. The cashier is an older woman and her attitude is about as stank as it can be. I pay for the purchase with the money mami gave me. I have to catch myself to keep from cussing her dumb ass out for snatching the money out of my hand. Lucky for her, I'm in the Christmas spirit and willing to spare her this verbal thrashing. And it hits me, like a ton of bricks. Shit, it hits me like a whole fucking building. I grab the grocery bag hurriedly, hustle toward the door hoping to catch the woman before she gets too far out into the parking lot.

"Shit Farah, slow down," I hear Clarissa holler after me.

My feet have already hit the pavement. I spot her pushing her basket across the walkway.

"Excuse me," I shout trying to get her attention.

Whoo, my fat ass needs to go to the gym, I think breaking into a light jog in her direction.

"Oh, did I forget something?" she asks, her expression confused.

Now that I can see her fully, I notice that she is extremely pretty. She is rather slim, not a curve or a bump to her. Poor thing don't have no kind of booty but her breasts are massive compared to her tiny frame. Her dark eyes are hidden behind a pair of black framed eyeglasses.

"I'm sorry," I pant. "This is probably awkward but I feel like I know you from somewhere."

I am lying horribly but she doesn't seem to notice. Instead, she laughs lightly, says, "Couldn't be me, I don't live around here."

Clarissa takes position beside me looking on with uncertainty.

"Oh."

"I'm from Delaware, just in town visiting for a few days."

"Is your name Lisa?"

She shakes her head no. "No, it's Tracy."

Despite standing outside in the blistering cold, I suddenly feel hot all over. My knees feel weak. If someone were to push me I would tip right over onto the ground.

I force a smile. "Well Tracy, you definitely have a twin. Sorry to have bothered you, enjoy your holiday."

"It's okay. Happy holidays, enjoy your Christmas too."

I stand in the middle of the parking lot watching her as she walks away; watch her as she puts her son, Elliott's son, in the back of her car.

"What the hell was that about?"

"Nothing," I stammer. "Lets go."

"Nah heffa, you look like you've seen a ghost."

"Something like that."

She grabs my arm forcefully turning me to face her. "Who was that woman, Farah?"

"Her name is Tracy and she is the ghost from Grayson's past."

"Are you going to tell him?"

I jump at the sound of Clarissa's voice. I am in a trance; my mind is off somewhere else.

"No," I mutter.

"The Farah I know would march right in that damn house and tell her man that she's just seen his ex-girlfriend prancing around Wal-Mart with his brother's son and wouldn't think twice away it."

Damn right I would...normally.

"I can't be that Farah tonight. I'm not just dealing with any ole man; I'm dealing with a wrecked man."

Flakes of snow are starting to fall slightly against the windshield. It's going to be a white Christmas for once.

"You're right. Forget I said that," Clarissa declares. "Do you think he knows she's here?"

"I don't know. It's the holidays and Elliott isn't spending it with us so it can only mean she's either here or Elliott is there. What are the odds of me running into her? Like really, just my fucking luck."

I groan burying my face in my hands. Running into her supersedes the trip around the world for cranberry sauce. I am absolutely miserable and now I have to go home and smile in my man's face like I didn't just share a conversation with the ex-love of his life.

"I'm going to tell him," I say with no conviction whatsoever.

Clarissa glares over at me. "You just said no two minutes ago! Leave it alone, okay. Lets not ruin the holiday for everyone."

I cross my arms over my chest with a pout. "Well the Clarissa I know would have told me fuck yeah, do that shit. The hell happened to you in two damn minutes?"

"We're all under *your* roof for Christmas this year which is a special occasion in itself. I would hate to ruin everyone's good fun with an unnecessary argument. Besides, you said so yourself. He cringes at her name. I'm pretty sure he doesn't want his mood ruined tonight. Go home and...ride him or something."

I huff, "Really Clare, that's your brilliant idea?"

She chortles. "What! I mean, it will take your mind off of it and it will damn sure make him happy. Everybody wins."

"You're no damn help. I mean none at all!"

I turn my head away from her, peering out of the window at the snow as it begins to pick up.

Clarissa sighs loudly. "No one needs a constant reminder of the fucked up shit going on in their lives. Let it go, at least until we get the hell out of dodge."

I have to shake my head at my sister. Sometimes I think she has a few bulbs missing in her building. Nonetheless, she is right. With a heavy sigh, I push the thoughts of my encounter with Tracy to the back of my mind.

I Yes

"Wake up, baby."

His soft kisses against the base of my ear wake me from my slumber. I can feel his hardness pressed firmly against my behind. I moan sleepily, say, "she's not awake yet."

I feel the vibrations of his laughter against my skin. "I'll wake her up," he replies in a playful, stifling tone.

The warmth of his hand ignites my flesh as he eases it between my legs forcing my thighs apart. He caresses me with slow, teasing circles. Around and around he moves until a finger eases inside of me, then two. I inhale loudly; clasp my bottom lip between my teeth trying ineffectively to muffle my moans.

"I think she's ready," he breathes wiggling out of his underwear. I am panty less and thankfully so considering they would be dampened by now.

He pulls my back to his chest palming my breasts in his hands. He lifts my leg over his and unhurriedly eases his length inside of me. My parents are in the bedroom down the hall. At this point, I could give two shits to the wind if they hear us or not. He smacks my ass roughly once and then again, grips my waist hard as he continues his relentless strokes. He pulls me in closer, so close like he is ready to crawl up inside of me. And when he hits that spot like the champ he is, I come around him. His name becomes the sweetest song to ever leave my lips.

Feet of snow have fallen over the city, it is a white Christmas. Inside, mami has the house alive with Christmas music by The Temptations and The Jackson 5. The floor to ceiling Christmas tree is decorated extravagantly with white lights and purple and silver ornaments and garland. Everyone is scattered about the floor pulling presents from under the tree, distributing them rightfully.

"You guys really didn't have to get me anything," Grayson says shyly as Clarissa pushes a fifth box in front of him.

"Oh shut up! As long as you are in my sister's life, you are apart of this family and gifts are included in the deal."

Before he met me, it had been years since he spent Christmas with anyone. He smiles forcefully. "Thanks sis."

Clarissa shoves a medium sized box into my hands. It's perfectly wrapped with my name written across it in impeccable cursive.

"That's real fancy," mami gushes. "Open it up, lets see what it is."

Anticipating eyes watch as I meticulously pull apart the wrapping paper. Inside is a smaller black box with a gold bow around it. I pull at a piece of the ribbon unraveling it so that I can take the top off. Inside of this box is a logoed *Tiffany's* box, much smaller than the one it's sitting in. With shaken hands I pull it out, undo its bow and draw the top off. My breath catches in my throat at the sight of a 2.2ct, 14kt gold engagement ring.

"Oh my goodness!" Clarissa exclaims.

I'm speechless. Even if I had a cue card, I still wouldn't be able to find the words. My eyes fly in Grayson's direction. He's propped up on one knee smiling at me. The room is silent. My heart is racing in my ears; it feels like it's louder than the Christmas music playing through the speakers. He takes the box from my fingertips, pulls my hand into his.

"I really love you Farah Acosta. I love what you do to me, I love how you challenge me, I love your family...I love you. I need you. I know I'm not perfect and my life is pretty screwed up but you have accepted me in my rarest form. I can't tell you how much that means to me. When I asked you before, it just wasn't right for us. And you were correct; I was only trying to keep you the best way I could think of. This is different. I can't even envision myself without you. Even my dreams are no comparison to the reality of having you in my life."

He pauses attempting to clear the swelling in his throat. He wipes silent tears away with the back of his hand and every part of me crumples under the weight of my cry. I feel his words, deep down to the depths of my spirit. His eyes are beseeching, needing and wanting me the same as I do him.

"Please marry me Farah Acosta."

I am engulfed with emotions. It's not the fear of taking on everything that is attached to this man but the fear of spending the rest of my life with someone that consumes me. At some point, I questioned whether I was good enough for a man to ever love me again. I had dealt with so many dead end situations that I just stopped trying and began embracing the fact that I would be single for however long it would take to find someone new. Then I met Grayson, a man just as broken as I once was. And the love that I had been yearning to give to someone else was the exact type of love he needed.

With a face full of tears, I tell the man I love, "yes."

"Fight for what you love, let go of what you don't..."

Grayson Powell

ǀ The Other Side of the Game

"Yes Mr. Moore, I'll have the prints ready for you this week..."

A quick knock draws my attention to the door before a pair of thick legs in stiletto heels step inside. Her maroon colored dress is clinging to every curve, accentuating the protrusion of her behind. Her skin is flawless, radiant under light make-up and glossed lips. Her hair swept away from her face neatly hanging down the middle of her back. She smiles at me, a warm dimpled smile.

"Mr. Powell...Mr. Powell..."

"Oh yes, I'm sorry Mr. Moore," I stammer turning to look away. "What were you saying, we were breaking up."

"I'll send you an e-mail to set up a time to swing by and look over them."

"That sounds good; I'll be looking for it. Have a good day, Mr. Moore."

I disconnect the call just as Farah walks up behind my desk, stands between my legs invading me with her sweet scent.

"Good afternoon, Mr. Powell."

I sit up pressing my nose to the apex of her thighs wanting her, craving her. "Mm, Ms. Acosta."

She giggles, runs her hands across my hair. "I came to pick you up for lunch," she says.

I push my hand up the front of her dress; feel her lace panties underneath my fingertips. "I thought you meant *you* were lunch."

"Grayson..."

She tries to pull away from me but I catch her by the back of the thighs easing her panties down to her ankles, she no longer fighting me.

I shove stacks of papers to the side pushing her up onto the cold wood. Pressing her knees back to her shoulders, I devour her as if it's my last meal. Licking and sucking until I feel her legs tremble beneath my grip, hear her trying desperately to stifle her moans as she comes onto my tongue. It's the most alluring sound.

"Don't move," I tell her getting up to lock my office door.

In three easy moves, I'm exposed, hard and ready. "Shit," she hisses in my ear as push my way inside of her, my favorite place to be. I clasp a hand over her mouth moving feverishly feeling myself about to explode from this good feeling. She wraps her legs tighter around me, pulling me in deeper and I practically lose all self control. We come harmoniously at once and I'm just as satisfied as if I would have eaten a full course meal.

We call in orders at the local diner down the street and have it delivered to the office as a late lunch. I watch her practically inhale the cheeseburger and fries before I can even take my fork out of the plastic wrapping.

"Hungry?" I quiz with a raised eyebrow.

Embarrassed, she hides her mouth with a hand until she's finished chewing. "Sorry, I'm starving. I didn't get to eat breakfast this morning."

"It seems like you're always starving."

She frowns over at me. "Mr. Powell, are you insinuating something?"

"Honestly Farah, when was the last time we used condoms? You haven't been on birth control for well over a year. Maybe we should take a test. You know, just to be sure you're not pregnant."

"*We?* Last time I checked men can't piss on a stick, "she mutters sarcastically.

I roll my eyes, reply, "Actually we can piss on any damn thing we want to but you know what I meant, smart ass."

She stuffs the last piece of the burger into her mouth. "Fine," she grumbles between bites. "I'll take a stinking test."

She can be such a difficult woman but I love the hell out of her. If there is one thing I know about Farah, it is her body. I have noticed those ten pounds she has gained over the last two months. I have also noticed the period she missed that should have come three weeks ago. I keep my observations to myself and play along as if I know nothing.

I stare at the paragraph indicator blinking repeatedly waiting on me to type something, anything. I groan loudly resting my head in my hands, my elbows propped up on my desk. Somewhere between turning on the computer and opening up a blank document, I lost all motivation to do anything. If it's not a report, it's a blueprint. If it's not a blueprint, it's a meeting of some sort. Work has been consuming especially with us taking on a major project that is set to begin next month. The soft tap at the door pulls me from the tedious task and I'm immediately thankful for the distraction. Farah is standing there in a pair of shorts and a tank top, her nipples poking deliciously through the thin fabric.

"Sorry to bother you," she says stepping further inside.

"I wasn't getting anywhere fast, it's fine. What's up?"

She walks around my oversized desk and climbs into my lap. The sweet smell of her perfumed lotion is inviting, tantalizing even. Her damp hair is pulled into a messy ponytail. She looks up at me through dense grey eyes. For a few moments, a heavy silence settles over us.

"I took the test," she replies running her manicured fingers through my beard.

"I thought you were going to wait until the morning."

She sighs. "I was but I was too anxious to wait."

"And what's the verdict?"

I see the tears as they build up, escape down her cheeks.

"I'm pregnant."

I run my thumb under her eyes wiping away fallen tears. "Why are you crying? That's the best news I've heard all week."

"I'm scared, overwhelmed. You don't seem the least bit shocked."

I lean in, plant small kisses on the tip of her nose. "Why should I be?"

She punches me hard in the arm. "You knew, didn't you? That's fucked up Grayson, why didn't you tell me?"

I rub the spot where her punch landed, her heavy handed ass. "I am observant. I speculated but I didn't know for sure. I thought you would have figured it out after you missed your period."

Her face flushes with discomfiture. "I didn't even notice. I have been so consumed with work, Clarissa's baby shower; wedding plans...I hadn't even thought twice about it."

"I know. I am excited though. We get to start our own little family."

That makes her smile. "You're not scared at all?"

"Of course I am," I reply. "I wonder if I'll be a good father. Will I want to walk away from my kid, give him or her away?"

"Grayson," she snaps. "Stop it."

I exhale loudly. "I just want to make sure that I'm better than that."

"Of course you will be. Don't ever talk like that again. You're a great man and you're going to be an even better father."

"And you, a great mother."

She kisses me fully. "You are an amazing man and I love you very much."

"I love you too."

She yawns. "I'm tired. I feel better now that I have told you. I have been going back in forth in my head for the last hour about how I'm going to break the news. I'm happy that you're happy and now I can rest easy."

"I am very happy."

She stands up from my lap, stretches loudly. I slap her playfully on the ass. She grins, says, "Come to bed with me."

I look over at the computer; the indicator is still waiting on me to type my first words. "I really need to get some work done."

She pouts. "Please

"I won't be long, I promise." I smirk. "If you are sleep when I get upstairs, I'll *wake* you up."

She giggles. "I bet you will. I'll see you upstairs."

In a few months, our lives are going to change. It will no longer be just Grayson and Farah but *our* family under this roof. I'm excited yet fearful; being a parent is another job without the paycheck. The thought of Farah with a protruding belly and spread nose waddling around the house warms me, brings a smile to my face. And I find myself falling in love all over again.

1 Blast from the Past

I am cruising down the highway. My windows down enjoying the warm spring air as it whips around me. Robin Thicke's latest joint *Get Her Back* plays through the speakers. I turn the volume up a few notches and vibe to the track. My man Robin jacks up his whole marriage, writes an entire album about it, and still loses his wife. I guess he knows now fame and fortune isn't everything when you do a good woman wrong. I'm headed toward Alexandria to have lunch with Farah's father to discuss wedding arrangements. It's crazy how close he and I have become, how much like a *real* father I consider him to be. I ease off the exit, make two rights, and pull into their appealing community. The neighborhood kids are out playing at the park, people walking their dogs, it's a typical Saturday. Mrs. Acosta answers the door when I arrive. She's dressed in a pair of sweatpants and a t-shirt, her shoulder length hair pushed back into a ponytail. It's rare to see her this way. She is normally decked out from head to toe even when she is just sitting around the house. Nonetheless, she looks beautiful as always.

"Hey son," she says inching up on her tip toes to kiss me on the cheek.

I smile warmly. "Hey mom."

The smell of food and vanilla and jasmine scented candles greet me when I walk in. I hear The Temptations singing about papa being a rolling stone from the kitchen. "Go on in honey, Anthony is out back grilling."

Mr. Acosta is poking at a steak on the large gas grill when I step out onto the deck. He's dressed down in shorts and a t-shirt with dark sunglasses on his face sweating like a part-time slave.

"Hey, there you are. How do you like your steak?"

"Medium rare."

"That's what I'm talking! Have a seat; grab a beer out the cooler. How are things going?"

I pop open the top to the red cooler next to the grill and grab a cold beer, plop down onto one of the patio chairs, and kick my feet up. "I can't complain, Mr. Acosta. Business is good, Farah and I are great...it's all good on my end. What about you?"

"Same shit, the only thing that changes is the day. I must be the luckiest man in the world to have *two* grandchildren on the way."

I laugh. "Yes sir, we found out a few days ago."

"Things are certainly speeding along for you two, huh?"

I open my beer with the bottle opener on my keychain and take a swig, nod, and say, "Yeah, I guess it is."

He looks at me over his shoulder. "Fatherhood isn't easy, you sure you're ready for it?"

I scuff. "Well, this baby is coming so I have no other choice but to be ready. I'm as ready as I am going to get."

"You sound like Christian. I'll tell you like I told him: the moment you lay eyes on that child, your whole world is going to change. The only thing you are going to ever want to do is protect your child. Everything else falls right in line behind that thought. I love how well you treat my daughter. You are a great guy; I think you will make an even better father."

He smiles warmly at me.

"Thank you so much, that means a lot. I hope I am."

The patio door slides open and Mrs. Acosta steps out balancing a bowl of fresh salad in one hand and freshly mashed potatoes in the other.

"Let me help you with that..."

"Grayson, sit your ass down. I got it."

I laugh. "Yes ma'am."

She sets the bowls down on the table, strategically positioning them between the plates and cups. "That should do it. I think you two should be all set. I'm about to head up and get dressed so I can take my daughters shopping."

"With what money?" Mr. Acosta asks.

She steps up next to him sticking her hand out, palm up. "Yours so give it up."

He sucks his teeth, dips into his shorts pocket retrieving his wallet. He takes a moment to peruse the line of cards before pulling one out and handing it to her.

"Don't ya'll be out there spending up all my damn money now?"

"You worry about your steaks," she jokes snatching the plastic from his fingers. "I'll worry about the money."

She pulls his face into hers and kisses him deeply. "Thank you daddy."

I don't know whether I should be covering my eyes or taking notes.

He smacks her on the ass as she turns to walk away. *And that's how a real man does it*, I think scribbling observations into my mental pad.

She steps back inside. He looks over at me with a smirk, "I have to keep the misses happy so she can keep daddy happy."

I chuckle. "Duly noted."

After a few minutes, he places two succulent steaks onto a serving plate and sets them on the table next to the other food. I'm hungrier than a fat man at a buffet right now and everything on this table is looking like it was made in heaven's kitchen. We take seats at the table in front of empty plates, pile them high with food, pray over the hands that prepared it, and dig right in.

For a few minutes we humor ourselves with highlights from last night's game: the Oklahoma Thunder versus the New York

Knicks. I stop to take a drink from my beer, my second one thus far. Mr. Acosta takes that moment to reach into his pocket and pull out a folded piece of paper.

"Let me go ahead and give you this. This is the real reason why I wanted to meet with you today."

Confused, I open it revealing a check written out for five thousand dollars.

"What is this for?" I stammer.

He chuckles. "That is my contribution toward the wedding, an early gift from my wife and me."

"But sir...this practically covers the whole wedding."

His eyes widen with the fakest shock theater tickets can buy. "Well shit, look at that."

"Sir, this is way too gracious of you. I can't accept this."

He narrows his eyes at me. "Yes the hell you can! You won't mess up my newly purchased checks. It's a gift Grayson; it's a gift that is supposed to help create a memory for you and my daughter that will last a lifetime."

I sigh. I have no way of talking him out of this, his mind is made up. I stare at the check once more. His handwriting is better than some females I know. I know the old school tradition is the bride's family pays for the wedding but damn. I give it no more thought. It's not like I can do much about it anyway. I fold the check back up, pull out my own wallet, and stuff it inside.

"Thank you sir," I say humbly. "Thank you very much."

He smiles with satisfaction. "No problem...now back to that game."

It's shortly after six when I leave the Acosta's. Slightly buzzed from the four beers and two shots of Brandy I had, I decide I don't feel like sitting in the house since I know Farah is out somewhere blowing all of her father's dough with her mom. I take a detour to Elliott's house, a smooth ten minute ride down the highway. I sync my phone to my car's audio system, punch his number into my speed dial, and let it ring out through the speakers while I wait for him to answer. After a minute, it goes straight to voicemail. Taking the exit ramp to his apartment, I decide against calling him a second time. I see his car parked in its usual designated spot and assume he must be sleep or away from his phone. Mr. Edwards, the building's security guard, nods my way as I walk through the lobby of Elliott's apartment building toward the elevator.

"Grayson my man, how you been?"

"I've been living, Mr. Edwards. How are you?"

"I'm alright brother, I'm doing alright."

"That's good to hear. Have a good one."

"Same to you."

A catchy jazz tune plays softly from the speaker overhead as I ride the elevator up seven floors to his apartment. The smell of freshly vacuumed carpets greets me when I step off into the hallway. I knock boldly on the door, no answer. I almost knock a second time until I realize I have the spare key he gave me last year. I unlock the door and push it open. A set of familiar brown eyes peer at me from over his dark blue leather couch.

"Grayson!" she exclaims stumbling to her feet.

I freeze, I feel like I have just fallen into the twilight zone.

"Tracy," I say acidly. "What are you doing here?"

My heart speeds up, my stomach churns, and my blood starts to simmer all at once. I haven't seen this woman in years. She is still attractive as the first day I met her even though she has lost a good ten or fifteen pounds. Her eyes shift frantically from me to the partially opened door of Elliott's bedroom. "I...um..."

She's nervous under my fiery stare, about as nervous as a stripper on amateur night. Before she can push the words from her mouth, a half naked Elliott comes barreling from the bedroom.

"Hey, I heard....Grayson, what are you doing here?"

Break out the fucking balloons; it's a damn party in here.

"I came by to see you. I called but you didn't answer; now I see why."

"Don't be fucking silly," he snaps. "I was taking a shower."

My eyes still piercing into her, I ask, "What is she doing here?"

"This is really fucking great," he mumbles under his breath. "It's my son's birthday tomorrow; she came up so we can take him out to celebrate."

I turn to leave. "Grayson, please...wait."

The sound of her voice tears away at my heart and infuriates me all in the same breath. I am unnerved by her presence; I have avoided her for as long as I could. She is a ghost from my past, no longer haunting my thoughts but physical in presence.

"What do you want, Tracy?" I hiss.

"Please stop running away," she pleads. Her eyes full of sorrow, regret.

"You have got to be kidding me. I'm standing in a room with the woman that fucked my brother and you want me to just suck it up and be okay with that shit?"

She cringes underneath my words, tears pillow in her eyes. I am not fazed, not in the least. "The audacity of you to think I should be sympathetic to your situation and just forget all of it ever happened so everybody can be one big fucking happy family. Fuck you Tracy!"

"Watch your mouth, Grayson," Elliott retorts. "My son is sleeping in the other room, lower your damn voice."

"Of course, that's so damn rude of me. Fuck this, I'm leaving anyway. I guess this is what I get for not waiting to get you on the phone before I came. It's cool, this won't happen again."

Elliott calls my name but it is quickly muffled by the sound of the door slamming behind me. I don't wait for the elevator to come. I take the steps down to the lobby in an attempt to flee the worst of my past.

"Are you going to eat your dinner or you're just going to stare at it all night?"

Farah frowns over at me from across the dining room table, her grey eyes questioning. I shift, push the plate of lasagna and salad toward the middle of the table.

"I'm not hungry," I mumble.

She eases back against her chair, crosses her arms over her swelling breasts.

"You're full of shit," she says coldly.

I exhale loudly. "Farah, please...with your smart ass mouth."

"Do not *Farah please* me, Grayson. What's wrong with you?"

Resting my elbows on the table with my head in my hands, I rub my temples slowly. "Nothing...just some shit with my brother."

"So how is that nothing? Can you please talk to me, Grayson? I know you're not telling me everything. What is the matter?"

For once, I would love for her not to care. I would much rather she just say 'okay' and leave me be. That would be too much like right. That would be too much unlike Farah. It is not in her character to let anyone she loves or cares about sit in their emotions. It doesn't help that she is a counselor either. Sometimes I feel like she just doesn't know how to turn the shit off. Nonetheless, I know this conversation is not going to go well. That is what scares me. Why didn't I just go to the bar like I thought to? She would be sleep by the time I got home and I could have bypassed all of this shit. No. I thought I would feel better if I came home to Farah and saw her face, heard her voice. I was wrong, dead ass wrong. I groan. I don't want to have this conversation. I am desperately fishing for the words to tell this woman that I ran into the ex-love of my life just hours before. I can't even fake like she still doesn't make me feel some type of way. What the fuck is wrong with me? My head is starting to thump.

Jesus be some Advil!

"I really don't want to talk about this, please. Not right now."

With a raised eyebrow, she replies, "The last time you didn't want to talk about something, you dropped a helluva bomb on me later on."

I exhale loudly. *This woman!* "I ran into Tracy a few hours ago," I murmur.

I glance up at her. Her face is stone, her voice steady. It's a scary combination for any woman to have after telling her you saw your ex earlier that day.

"And?"

I swallow the lump in my throat. "I went to see Elliott after I left your parent's house just to catch up with him and she happened to be there. She came down to celebrate their son's birthday tomorrow."

She inhales sharply. "How did that make you feel?"

I feel like one of her clients laying on the chaise lounge in her office. That's how the hell I feel!

"Angry," I answer. "She spoke to me...told me I need to stop running...how in the fuck am I supposed to act?"

"She's right."

"What the fuck did you say?"

Before the words have fully left my mouth, I regret saying them. Her eyes burn with a fury I cannot even begin to describe. She is no longer the counselor Farah. Her understanding has jumped out the window, her patience thin as the wind.

"First of all Grayson Michael Powell, don't talk to me like that! You have no reason to be angry with me, I did nothing to you. Second of all, how long are you going to keep ducking and dodging this situation? It's not going to go away...it's *never* going to go away. I don't want you coming into our marriage still harboring ill emotions toward them."

"You don't get it!"

"I don't get it," she hollers bewildered. "Seriously?! What is there not to get? Your ex-girlfriend, the love of your fucking life sleeps with your brother and gets pregnant. I get that. Instead of seeking some type of closure, instead of sitting down and talking about it, you find it better to run away. I get that. That woman can still rile up emotions in you that should *not* be there. I fucking get it! Did I miss something there? Have I covered it all?"

"Enough Farah, I don't want to have this argument with you," I snap pushing up from my seat.

"Don't you dare walk out of this room? I will not let you run away from this conversation. How can you possibly love me the way you say you do, want to be with me like you claim if this is still haunting you? You want to marry me and I'm not taking any prisoners. I will not aid you in holding grudges against people. You decide how you want to live your life. You have a woman that loves you unconditionally and a child coming into this world that will love you just as much. Let that past situation go. You don't have to forget...you'll never forget it but sometimes you just have to forgive people for the sake of *you*."

The metal clinks against the table top. In an instance, my world spirals down around me. It is a crushing feeling.

"There will be no wedding," she says through tears. "No wedding until you get your shit together. I love you so much and you have no idea how hard this is for me. No idea! I will not come in second to your past. You told her it would be okay to have that baby. That connects her and Elliott for life and it is something you have to live with too. To see how discombobulated this woman has you really hurts, Grayson. The wedding is *off.* She won, I can't compete."

I hear her socked footsteps near me, my back toward her. She brushes past me never looking back. I want to reach out and stop her, fall to my knees and beg for her forgiveness. I can't, my body is numb. Instead, I watch her walk up the steps, her stomach rounding from the little person growing inside of her. The room around me becomes blurry and I realize I'm crying.

| A Different Kind of Love

My eyes are bloodshot. I haven't slept all night long. I lie on the pull-out couch staring up at the ceiling. What once was night is now turning into morning. I don't know the time; I haven't even bothered to check. I hear her bare feet against the wooden floor in the foyer as she nears the living room. A few moments later, I feel the mattress dip and move beside me. The scent of her hair and lotion whirls around me, tugs at my emotions. She lifts the comforter, eases on top of me resting her breasts against my chest.

Her voice cracks as she says, "I love you Grayson."

The tears I once hid, I am unable to hide any longer as they slide down the sides of my face and settle into the pillow underneath my head. When she looks at me, it makes my heart constrict even more. Her expression is melancholy; swollen grey eyes look down on me. For the second time, this is what I have done to her. I feel like a failure. She reaches up cupping my head in her hands, runs her thumb across my face wiping away my tears. She settles her lips against mine. Her kiss is soft and comforting.

"You might as well leave me," I utter.

The thought is as painful as the words leaving my mouth.

"Leave you? I am not going anywhere, Grayson. I don't give up that easily. I am sorry for the things I said last night. I was being selfish…"

"You have every right to be. You're right, why should you marry a man who is still affected by someone he used to love. That's not fair to you. What am I supposed to do? How do I get over someone that really hurt me?"

"Talk to her. I know it sounds crazy coming from me but there's nothing else you can do if you don't get it off of your chest, baby."

I sigh. "Yeah, it does sound crazy coming from you. That doesn't bother you, me sitting down and talking to her?"

She cocks her head to the side, furrows her eyebrow. "Is it supposed to? Do you still love her or something? Would you like to spring something else on me?"

"No….hell no. That love died years ago."

"You know sometimes you can talk yourself right into a hole, Grayson."

I chuckle lightly. "I'm starting to realize that. The only woman I love is you. I only ask because I know how women can be and…I don't know. Forget I said that."

"I don't feel the need to be nervous, bothered, fearful, or any emotion equating to those. I want you to get this shit over with so we can move on with our lives. That's it. She can come incorrect if she wants to. I have no problems tapping her skinny ass, pregnant and all."

I frown up at her. "Calm down thug thizzle, how do you know she is skinny?"

"Wild guess," she says with not a piece of conviction in her voice.

"Wild guess, my ass. Answer the question."

She sighs as if kicking herself in the ass. "When mami sent Clarissa and me to the store for cranberry sauce on Christmas Eve, I ran into her. Her son has those eyes just like you and Elliott and I knew...I knew who she was before I even asked her name."

"Why didn't you tell me?"

"For what? So you can act the way you did last night? Why stir up emotions if I don't need to. Are you mad?"

"I understand. I'm not mad."

If there is anything I am in this moment, it's horny. She is been lying on my penis for well over twenty minutes and I am aching to explore her. I dip my fingers into her hair; lean up capturing her lips with mine. She eases into it greeting me with her tongue. A moan rumbles from her throat, pulls the beast from its slumber. Careful not to crush her with my weight, I roll over on top of her settling between her thighs. I take a moment to admire her. I am grateful to have a woman that will endure this battle with me. Many are not so lucky.

"You always did have this staring problem," she says jarring me from my thoughts.

I smile. "Just thinking about how much I love you. You are a beautiful woman. I have always told you that, Farah Elise."

She reaches down within the space between our bodies cupping my softness in her palm. Blood begins to thump through that part of me, swells at the beckoning from the warmth of her hand. I smother her with my kisses; rub my now hardened penis against that hot spot I know is waiting for me. She purrs in my ear as I undress her enough to ease myself inside of her. Her warmth, her wetness draws me in deeper. I make love to her losing myself inside of her as a means to escape my fucked up reality. When she touches me, my tears build and release. From the way she kisses me, I know we will be okay. Amidst all of my fuckedupness, she understands.

It's a Wednesday evening. I'm sitting in my home office in complete silence with my good friend Hennessey. It has been a long week and I haven't been much of myself since the incident Saturday. Tonight Farah is out of the house having dinner with her sister. Though the invitation to join was extended to me, I declined with an excuse of needing to get some reports done. Truth be told, I just don't want to be around too many people right now. My mind is still clouded. Farah's ring still sits on the dining room table, unmoved. She refuses to put it on and with good reason, I know. My cell vibrates against the wooden desk. It's Elliott.

I exhale, answer, "Hello."

"Hey Grayson, how are things going?"

He sounds his normal self, surprisingly. After my acting debut in his living room, I at least expect him to be frustrated with me. I guess not.

"I've had better days."

"Lets get together and talk, I'm close by."

"Sure, just use your key to get in."

Five minutes later, I hear Elliott's dress shoes thud against the carpet in the living room before he appears in the doorway.

"Close by, huh?" I say sarcastically.

He chuckles lightly coming in to sit down. "I lied. I was already on my way here. You look rough bro."

"I know."

"Farah called me," he replies.

"Really?"

"She's worried about you. She wants you and Tracy to talk, clear the air. I've never seen Farah cry and frankly I'm glad, hearing it hurts enough."

I sigh loudly clenching my eyes shut at the thought of my fiancé in tears on the phone with my brother. "I'm sorry about that."

"You shouldn't be sorry. She's a good woman and she loves you very much. I'm kind of shocked she even wants you and Tracy in the same room with each other let alone talking."

"Scary, isn't it."

He scuffs, "like a got damn horror movie."

My head is beginning to throb. The same reoccurring headache I've been babying all week. I pull open the top desk drawer retrieving a bottle of *Tylenol*. I pop two pills washing them down with a swallow of Hennessey.

"Can I ask you something?"

"Yeah, shoot," he says leaning back in the winged chair across from my desk, his right foot resting on his left knee.

"Why is it so much easier for me to forgive you than her?"

He stills, eyes move around nervously and I know I have caught him off guard.

After a moment, he replies, "Double standards."

I lean forward, curious. "Do explain."

"You love me because I am your brother, your family. Even though I should have known better considering our relationship, she receives the brute of the situation because your love for her is different. Men have this fucked up way of thinking that men are men and it's expected of us to do some fucked up shit but the women should be the ones to make better decisions."

He pauses to retrieve a glass from the mini bar tucked away in a corner beside the floor to ceiling bookcase. He pours himself some brown poison before taking his seat once again.

"You're born into this relationship with me so it's almost like our love for one another is by default. I'm your brother, you will never have another. When you have to build trust and develop feelings which eventually turn into love for someone, it's a whole other ball game. They are pushed up on a higher pedestal. You trusted her with your heart and to a man, that's the most fragile thing we possess. If that shit is broken, it takes us years, if ever, to recover."

I sigh loudly. "Oh. So that's what it is?"

Elliott shrugs. "I think so. I wasn't thinking when I took it there with Tracy and I have never truly forgiven myself for what I've done to you. It's a hard pill to swallow and I live with it every day, every time I look at my son. I'm constantly reminded of how much of a fucked up brother I am and how our relationship will never be the same because of it. It was hard without you and I'm more than grateful that you accepted me back into your life. You and Tracy don't have to be best friends but at least put everything out on the table and let it go. You have a new life ahead of you, an amazing woman and you may not think so but you owe Farah that much too."

I groan at the thought of having to face Tracy again.

"I just want Farah to put her fucking ring back on. It's bothering me."

"I guess you'll be having that talk with Tracy, huh?"

I cut my eyes at him. "Do I have any other choice?"

He frowns, shakes his head no.

"Fuck! I really wish I could say this wasn't happening to me right now. I don't want to see her again. I don't want to hear her voice or even talk about this shit."

"It's your choice but consider what you could lose behind it."

"And then there is *that*, the possibility of losing the best thing to happen to me in years. I cannot let that happen, I cannot ruin my family bro."

"She will be back in a few weeks. You two can talk then, okay."

My head is banging like the Bloods and Crips.

"Fine, I just want to stop talking about this shit."

Elliott swallows back the remaining liquor in his glass. "I need to get going anyway; I have some work I need to finish up. I really just wanted to drop by and chat for a few."

"Hey baby!" Farah pokes her head through the door, her smile as bright as the sun that has already settled for the day. "Oh. Hey Elliott, I'm sorry to interrupt."

She's still looks like five o'clock wearing her business by day, dinner by night black dress with a pair of black and white pumps. Her long hair pushed back into a neat bun. The sight of her makes my heart run around in my chest like a marathon winner.

"Hey sis, it's cool I was just leaving."

She and Elliott exchange a brief hug. He looks back at me over his shoulder. "I love you bro and I will be in touch with you."

"Thanks. I love you too, have a good night."

"Are you okay?" she asks still lingering by the door.

"I'm fine, baby. Come here."

Her heels sink into the plush carpet as she moves toward me. I pull her close resting my large hands over her small bump. "How was dinner?"

She runs her fingernails across my neck and shoulders. A chill races through me. "It was nice. She brought Aiden along; he's such a good baby."

I push the hem of her dress up exposing her bare belly. I press my lips to her warm flesh.

"I love you...I love *her*."

Her voice spikes in surprise. "Her?"

"I want a girl."

"I do too. Lets hope you had good aim."

I smile. "Let that be one thing I've done right."

"Stop it."

"I'm sorry."

She carts away from me wiggling her dress back down over her hips. "I'm going to take a shower, join me."

I rise to my feet, filling the space between us. I'm so close to her I can feel her heart thumping against my stomach. "That's the best thing I've heard all day."

Her mouth pulls up into a smirk.

"Considering the fact that you have been cooped up in this office all day..." She pauses glancing down at the nearly empty bottle of Hennessey. "...and drinking nonetheless, you need it."

"You sound like you're judging me, baby."

Mockingly, she says, "Of course not, why on earth would I do that."

She eases up onto her tip toes, flexes her hips against my growing erection. I feel her breath on the base of my ear and my whole body tenses with a sexual yearning. She trails her tongue across my earlobe, presses her lips to that sensitive spot she knows drives me insane.

"You have five minutes to clean up and meet me upstairs."

She saunters off, her wide hips swaying from side to side.

My goodness, this woman!

ı Souls Intertwined

I watch her attentively as she stands in the doorway of our large walk-in closet peering at the rows of hung clothes with a frown. She's in a pair of black lace boy shorts and a black bra, her belly protruding with new life. In another month, we will find out if our little girl is *really* a girl or a boy. I think I am more excited than Farah at this point. It's a beautiful June day, doomsday it seems like. Two long months have come down to this very day, the day I will finally have my talk with Tracy. I'm reluctant, anxious to get it over with.

"Baby, you don't have to get flashy," I say nonchalantly watching her finger a dark purple dress before pushing it to the side. "We're just sitting down to talk."

Her lack of a response lets me know I am better off talking to a brick wall. Her back still turned toward me, she continues pushing hanger after hanger to the side. I didn't want Farah apart of this. I thought it would be best if just the three of us sat down and talked out our differences. Nope. Elliott thought it would be a good idea having Farah mediate with her being a counselor and all. Knowing Farah the way I do, one word can take the conversation left and I am just praying that doesn't happen.

"Would you like for me to go down there with this on?" she mutters retreating from the closet with a pair of royal blue Chuck Taylors. "I want to look presentable, Grayson. Is that so wrong?"

I glower. "With sneakers?"

She shrugs with a grin. "Reinforcement."

I cross my arms over my chest, glare at her. "Farah, you are not about to fight this woman. You are pregnant for goodness sake."

With every ounce of seriousness she can muster, she looks at me, and says, "And? You can't hit her but I sure do have a mean right hook. Grayson, I am not looking for a fight. I hope we can all sit down like adults and get through this but I am not stupid either. I don't trust too many women, she is one of them."

My inner self throws his hands up in defeat. *Just let it go Grayson, you are not going to win this.*

"Just put something on other than that," I grumble.

"Real cute," she huffs throwing the sneakers in the floor then turning back toward the closet. "I know somebody that likes it."

I hop off of the edge of the bed, ease up behind her, and grab her gently by the hips pinning her butt to the seat of my pants.

"I love it," I tell her.

She licks her lips seductively. "I see."

I am thankful for the shift in conversation. I slide my hand down into her panties; push a digit inside of her. She moans delightfully moving her hips in small circles against the palm of my hand. I tip my head back, my mouth gaped hardening from the friction of her ass rubbing against me. She's saturated. I don't know what it is about sex with Farah but I find myself feigning for her daily. She is enough to satisfy my hungry and quench my thirst! She pulls away from me, my finger drenched with her sweetness. She takes my hand in hers bringing it to her mouth, easing my wet finger inside. She's the *real* MVP. She grins at me as if satisfied with the taste. My breathing turns shallow. She starts to move forcing me backwards toward the bed while her fingers work at the buttons of my jeans. They fall in a heap around my ankles. She pushes me back against the bed. I love it when she takes control like this. Gracefully, she pulls my erection from my boxers covering it with the warmth of her mouth. An unashamed moan stirs in my throat; I grab a handful of her curls firmly in my grip. Taking me wholly in and out of her mouth at a teasingly slow pace, she pulls a world shattering orgasm out of me in the matter of minutes. And as if nothing ever occurred, she goes back to the closet to look for an outfit.

Her eyes are fixed on the wall behind me occasionally drifting over in my direction. It is so quiet; you can practically hear paint dry. I don't know which is worse: the deafening silence or being in the same room as Tracy again. She shifts nervously in her chair, clears her throat loudly.

"I'm so sorry I am late. I got caught up on an emergency call with a client."

Farah rushes into the room leaving behind a lingering scent of amber and coconut. I sigh with relief at the break in silence. She has settled on a backless flowing, beige sundress. Her hair falls in waves around her shoulders and down the length of her back. She is bare faced with just a hint of gloss on her lips. She has never needed makeup to define her beauty. In this instance, she looks amazing in her rarest form.

"Hello Tracy. My name is Farah. It's nice meeting you...again."

She holds her hand out to be shaken. Tracy takes it acceptingly, her expression perplexed.

"Again?" she quizzes.

"You may not recognize me but I met you a few months ago at Wal-Mart...around Christmas Eve."

Tracy's eyes widen with shock. "Yes, in the parking lot! Oh my goodness, yes I do remember. Why didn't you say something?"

Farah forces a nervous smile, sinks down into the chair at the head of the table.

"I didn't really know how to say it," she admits. "It's not exactly a conversation piece. It's pretty awkward."

Tracy's gaze settles on Farah's belly. "Oh, you're pregnant. Congratulations."

Her tone is dry, wounded.

"Thank you."

Grey eyes shift in my direction. Farah smiles comfortingly but it doesn't help to take the edge off of the situation.

"Uh...where should we start?" Elliott rubs his palms against his khaki shorts. He looks from me to Tracy then at Farah, questioningly.

"I can treat this like one of my sessions or you can talk amongst yourselves. Either way, I am just here to mediate."

There is more silence and we are back is this battle of who speaks first.

"Okay, so we are not getting anywhere fast doing this," Farah says after a few moments. "Session it is. How about we start with you Tracy? I mean, the main reason we are here is to hear from you anyway. I think the big question to be answered is why. That is where the clarity lies; that is where closure comes in."

Her eyes are fixed on Tracy, blazing with curiosity. Our stares follow, greedy for information. Tracy runs an unnerved hand over her hair.

"There really is no why," she says. "It just...it just happened."

Farah's face falls, her lips pursed. "Of course there is a why. Cheating doesn't just happen. There is a reason behind it, something in your brain says this is okay and you believe it. If even for a moment, you believe it. Spilling something *just* happens but cheating does not."

"I don't know what to tell you," Tracy says flatly. "If you ask me, it just happened. The why is the least of the problem right now?"

"So enlighten us...what is the *real* problem?"

I can hear the irritation in Farah's voice and I am most relieved she has decided to keep the sneakers upstairs.

"I just want Grayson to be a part of his nephew's life. Jaime knows who he is and he asks about him all the time. I am tired of making empty promises to my son. I want to fix that if nothing else."

"Tracy, realistically, you cannot want anything if you have not addressed the lingering issue between you two. He may not have verbally said it but he wants closure and he needs it. *We* need it. This is the man I am going to marry in a few months and..."

"Marry?"

"Yes marry," Farah says coolly.

I notice the ring is no longer sitting on the table. Instead, it's perched on her finger. I reach out and touch her hand, fiddle with the diamond. My inner little person does the running man. *Finally!*

She blushes, continues, "It's not the greatest table discussion but I think, and Elliott agrees, it needs to be had. "

"Fine," Tracy snaps shifting in her seat once more. "Lets talk Grayson."

I assume our display of affection has left her uncomfortable.

"It was supposed to just be a meeting to plan a surprise birthday party for you. I was supposed to be meeting with Elliott and his wife one night to get the arrangements in order but something happened and she went out of town on a whim. We met up after work. He offered me some drinks and we ordered food. No big deal. It wasn't until after the fifth drink that I started seeing Elliott differently. I can't say he wasn't looking good in his work clothes."

I grimace at her words. I am beginning to regret this meeting. Just when I thought I was ready to hear the truth, reality sets in.

"You ran around for the longest time hating your brother but the truth is I initiated everything. I made the first move and had Elliott been in his right mind, he probably would have stopped me. But he didn't and we ended up having sex. Needless to say, the awkwardness of the situation prevented us from ever coming together to throw you that party. It was that night that I got pregnant. We only had sex one other time and it was after you and I had had a spat and I walked out of the house. I drove around for hours, frustrated. I called Elliott crying and he met me in the parking lot of some restaurant. We did it in my car. I guess if we've done it once, what more damage it can do if you do it again. When I found out I was pregnant, I prayed to God that the baby was yours. My gut told me otherwise."

"Was it worth it?"

My blood is torrid through my veins, anger building.

Her voice falls. "No, it wasn't. Despite our indifferences from time to time, I had a really good thing and I fucked it up. Nothing was worth losing you over, Grayson."

"If she would have never gotten pregnant, do you think it all would have been easier to handle?" Farah asks me.

She reaches over and squeezes my hand. I feel like a tamed beast under her touch.

"Yes, I probably would have never found out about it. But it didn't happen that way and if it had, I would have never met you."

"So why urge her to have that baby. I'm not saying abortion is the correction solution but you had a firm hand in that decision, the ball was in your court..."

"I wasn't thinking, at least not about myself. I told you this."

Her voice is calm, soothing. "I know what you told me baby but I want you to tell them."

I can't bear to look at Tracy so I shift my attention to Elliott instead.

"I don't like abortion and as much as it hurt, even now, I thought it was the best thing for her to do. I didn't think it would affect me like this down the line. I thought that eventually I would get past it and move on and think nothing of it. My anger towards Tracy has festered inside of me. I loved her so much. I wanted a family with her, a child with her and she betrayed me."

Farah moves her hand back to her lap. I see the discomfort on her face. I hate that she has to hear this.

"I'm sorry, Farah," I mumble.

She forces a smile my way. "It's okay."

"It's very obvious you love her," Tracy utters barely above a whisper. "Way more than you ever did with me. She's beautiful, I can see why."

"It's not about looks," I tell her. "You have no idea how much this woman loves me, how patient she has been with me because of scars you left behind. That's something you will never be able to see. I have run away from this situation for as long as I could. She is here with me facing the music. That speaks volumes. So please, lets not sit here and compare levels of love."

Her eyes move back to the blank wall.

I redirect my attention to Elliott, ask, "Do you love Tracy?"

Without hesitation, he says, "Of course I do. The way any respectable man loves the mother of his child. I can never love Tracy the way you do Farah. I told myself after everything happened, I could never hurt you in that way again. We are good friends. We come together strictly to co-parent and nothing else."

"I can respect that," I conclude.

"Let me just say this..."

Tracy leans forward resting her elbows on the table. Her eyes secured on me. She wants me to look at her but I won't. When she finally realizes this, she continues, "For the longest time, I believed we would eventually get back together. I thought our love was strong enough to get us through this tough time. It was a foolish idea but I latched on to it for as long as I could. Eventually, I came to the conclusion that it was finally over and all because I had fucked up. I am very much regretful for what I did to you, Grayson. I can't see I feel comfortable sitting in a room with your fiancé but the reality of it is clear: you have moved on. You have a great life now and I wish you nothing but the best. Family is everything and I just want you to be a part of my son's life. Elliott wants it too; he talks about it all the time."

"I just always wondered why. What did Elliott have that I didn't? What did I do to make you want to take it there with him forfeiting our relationship? I felt like something was wrong with me for the longest time. You came into my life after I had gone through an elongated period of sleeping with every attractive Jane. You made me believe in love again and then you destroyed that image. You made me feel like every woman after you would do the same thing. I dated a few women here and there before Farah and I always let them go before they could hurt me. It was like I knew deep down some shit was about to happen and I wanted to crush their worlds before they did mines. It's an ugly thought process to have but I owe that all to you."

"No offense, but there isn't anything he had over you. It was just a really bad decision I made and I have lived and learned from it. I'm sorry, Grayson. I truly am. I know those words probably don't matter much now but I have had years to deal with it and I am most regretful for destroying a genuine man."

She wipes silent tears away with the back of her hand.

"With this entirely said, can we effectively move on from here for the sake of the little boy?" Farah asks.

"I would like to," Tracy answers.

Elliott chimes in, "I would like to as well."

For a moment, I think of all the women I hurt after Tracy; all of the declarations of love and the tears that followed because I didn't feel the same. For years, I have given Tracy control over my life by allowing what was done to me to be a reflection of what I did to others. When I realized I wasn't getting anywhere fast by doing so, I opened myself up and found a good thing in the form of a pure heart with grey eyes. I didn't need this meeting but I wanted it. I wanted to hear the things that I never did years ago. Frankly, it hurts those more knowing what they did to a good person than it does for me to forgive. I partly wanted the closure. More than anything, I want to be included in my nephew's life without harboring resentment for the decisions his parents made. Sometimes without getting the answers to the questions we have constantly asked ourselves after being hurt, we harbor it. I held on to it like it was doing me some good. I hid my past from Farah; I held a grudge against her unknowingly. I marked her the way I had every other female until I couldn't stop myself from falling in love with her any longer. Even then, I doubted that she might hurt me just as Tracy had. That is what happens to a man done wrong, the end result of a scorned heart.

"Yes, I am ready to put this behind me once and for all."

Tracy stands to her feet pushing the strap of her purse over her shoulder. "If we are done here, I need to be going."

Sensing the familiar ineptness creeping back into the room, Elliott replies, "Uh...yeah, it looks like we are. I will walk you out."

She smiles forcefully in Farah's direction. "It was nice seeing you again, Farah. You two enjoy your night."

I watch her disappear from the room. Four souls have intertwined; my past has come full circle with my present. I have faced the one woman I have held so much bitterness toward and she has done nothing but helped me appreciate the blessing I have in Farah.

"Well, I think that went okay. I didn't even have to use my reinforcement."

I laugh. "I thought you left them upstairs."

Farah winks at me, chuckles. "Oh no baby, they're in the hallway. A real lady is *always* ready."

"I love you and there are no *secrets* about that…"

– *Mr. and Mrs. Powell*

—

1 Woman to Woman

I stare blankly at a diagram of the different development stages of a baby during pregnancy. Grayson and I sit in complete silence waiting for Dr. Simmons to come in. Today is the day we find out the sex of our baby. I am anxious to receive the news and from the way Grayson is twiddling his thumbs, I can tell the feeling is mutual. The door of the examining room swings open and Dr. Simmons steps inside. She is a middle aged black woman with big brown eyes and large lips. Her skin is the color of cocoa and today she has her natural curls pulled back into a ponytail.

"Thank you for waiting, I'm sorry about the delay." She pauses reading our expressions. "Don't look so nervous you two."

I smile forcefully. "We're trying not to be."

"Well I won't keep you waiting any longer, lie back for me on the table please."

I do as I am told struggling against the weight of my belly to get my legs up and over onto the table.

Dr. Simmons lifts my shirt up exposing my bare stomach. "You look great, I must say. Since I last saw you, you have only gained about five pounds. You are maintaining a healthy weight for your baby so that's perfect."

The thought of looking like a blimp is not very appealing to me. I frown. Dr. Simmons laughs, says, "Trust me, Ms. Acosta, you can't even tell on you."

As if that makes me feel any better.

She spreads a clear liquid onto the monitor. "You know how this goes, Ms. Acosta. You're going to feel the coldness of the liquid for a brief moment, ok."

I nod bracing myself as she rests it against my flesh. She moves the monitor around in search of our baby. Our child is balled up sleeping peacefully. The steadiness of its heartbeat echoes throughout the room.

"The heartbeat is normal. Let me try to get in just a little bit more and see what we have in here."

I don't know whose heartbeat is louder, my baby's or my own pumping wildly in my ears. Grayson reaches over and grabs my hand, links his fingers through mine.

"And it looks like mommy and daddy is having a baby girl."

The news is joyous, whether boy or girl I would have been ecstatic as long as our baby is healthy. The thought of a mini-me is overwhelming. My emotions seize me quick bringing on tears. Grayson pulls my hand up to his lips kissing the back of it softly.

"I'm so happy," he says, his own eyes threatened with tears. "How lucky is the man to have two of you?"

Pretty fucking lucky, I think.

It's not a question that requires an answer. I paint a picture in my mind of what she will look like: big, bright grey eyes with a dimpled smile and lots of hair. I will dress her in cute little outfits, paint her room colors of lilac and yellows, and brush her hair back into decorative bows and barrettes. As much as Grayson stays glued to my belly always talking to her, she will probably be a daddy's girl just like me. I am happy and maybe that is too plain of a word to describe it.

He leans down and kisses me gently, says in between kisses, "I love you, Mrs. Powell."

The way he looks at me makes my insides melt, so much happiness and passion behind his eyes. And in this moment, I don't know who is luckier: him or me.

It's another Indian summer, a pregnant woman's worst nightmare. Aside from not being able to fit shit in my closet, I have to deal with being uncomfortably hot every time I walk out the door. Not to mention, my hair is growing like a weed from the prenatal vitamins and I am two seconds from chopping the shit off. I am in my car headed to work, windows rolled up with the air conditioning blaring. I'm running late as usual, too busy trying to squeeze my stomach in a dress I know won't fit. I finally settle on a peach sundress after thirty unproductive minutes of trying to find something to wear. It's a Thursday morning and I can't say I am not happy tomorrow is Friday. The week has been a busy one. I feel like I have seen more clients this week than I have in my whole entire career as a counselor. I pull into my designated parking spot; take a moment to apply a fresh coat of lip gloss before climbing out. I gather my briefcase from the backseat; struggle to reach some of the loose files that have shifted into the floor during my drive here.

"Excuse me...Farah."

My heart practically jumps out of my chest as Tracy nears my car. I don't know whether to be confused or glad I didn't have a damn heart attack.

"Jesus girl, you scared the hell out of me."

She gives me a coy smile. "Sorry about that."

I put a hand to my chest; take a few deep breaths in an attempt to gather my composure. "It's fine. What are you doing here? Wait...how do you know where I work?"

She looks like she is up to something, her demeanor is strange. I grip the handle of my briefcase tighter. She can try some shit if she wants to, I'll swing this damn briefcase and crack her ass upside the head with it.

Calm down pistol starter with your pregnant self, see what she wants first.

"The internet," she stammers. "I put your name in Google and the website for your counseling firm came up."

"Oh," I say dryly.

"I...um...want to talk to you and Elliott wouldn't give me your number so I had to find some other way to get in touch with you."

I wonder why. "Well...I guess you can come on up and we can talk in my office."

She gives me a perturbed smile before following me toward the front door. "Thank you, I would appreciate that."

"Good morning, Ms. Acosta." The security officer, Jerry, smiles at me with his always contagiously happy go lucky self.

"Good morning Jerry."

He nods at Tracy as she shuffles nervously behind me. The ride up to the office is both silent and awkward. I stand close to the button panel avoiding all eye contact with her. Inside, I sigh with relief once the doors open up to the fifth floor landing where the office is located. Through the double glass doors, I can see Erin cradling the receiver of the office phone between her shoulder blade and ear while she types something into the computer.

"Yes ma'am. I will make sure she gets the message. You have a wonder day."

Her eyes light up at the sight of me. "Good morning Farah. That color looks amazing on you."

"Thank you Erin."

She places the receiver back on the base, her eyes settle on Tracy. "Can I help you ma'am?"

"No, she's with me," I tell her. "This is Ms. Tracy and I will be meeting with her for a little bit this morning. If anyone calls just let them know I am in a meeting."

"Will do."

The stretch of the hallway to my office seems longer today. I stop to poke my head in Cathy's office. She's typing conscientiously on her computer; I knock to make my presence known.

"Good morning Cathy."

"Good morning Farah! Girl, I don't know if it's that baby or Grayson that has you glowing but you are radiating."

I giggle. "Thank you. I'm going to be meeting with someone for a little bit so I will have to push our daily meeting back, okay."

"Sure thing, just buzz me when you're ready."

Tracy stirs impatiently.

"You're a busy woman," she says.

Well bitch what do you think I'm supposed to be? I'm at work!

I wish she wasn't acting so damn awkward right now. It's unnerving.

"Have a seat," I reply motioning toward one of the winged chairs once we are inside of my office. I move toward the window drawing the curtains to let the sunlight beam through. Her eyes travel my wall of plaques, certificates, and degrees. She seems thoroughly impressed.

"This is nice."

"Thank you. Can I get you anything, coffee or water maybe?"

She plops into the chair. "No thank you."

I settle into my own chair, thankful to finally have some room between us. "So what can I do for you?"

"I know the last time we met; it wasn't exactly a happy occasion. I figured since Grayson and I have smoothed everything over, you and I should speak woman to woman."

"Why would we need to do that?" I blurt out.

"Jamie is going to be around you now and our families are going to be coming together so I figured we should get to know each other better."

At nine o'clock in the morning?

"Forgive me, Tracy if what I am about to say may sound rude," I huff. "You show up to my job out of the blue because you think we need to get to know each other now that you and Grayson are *semi-cordial*? Let's keep it funky, what is the real reason you came here because I am not buying what you are telling me right now?"

Her whole demeanor changes; I mean, everything about her does a whole 360.

"I'm not fully comfortable with my son being around you," she says coolly. "I can't be anymore honest than that. Even after all of these years, I still have some feelings for Grayson and I'm not okay with my son being around my ex's new wife. And because I'm not comfortable I think we need to *get* comfortable with one another first."

"New wife?" I snap. "I am his *only* wife. You are speaking like I'm about to be married to Elliott. Get comfortable? If you don't want me around your child, that's fine. Let me make something crystal clear honey, my husband will not be in your presence without me. So it seems like we have yet another issue on our hands, don't we."

She grimaces. "Is that really how it is going to go, Farah? All I ask is that we get rightfully acquainted with one another since my son is going to be around you now."

I don't like her tone of her voice. I'm not feeling anything about her right now. My smack-a-bitch hand is throbbing and I am trying desperately to hold it together.

"I would have never had an issue with Grayson being around you; in fact, you pose no threat to my relationship in any form or fashion. But when you walk into my office being nasty with me because you can't handle the fact that he has someone else in his life, I have to shut shit down."

She raises an eyebrow at me. *The nerve of this bitch!*

I continue, "Elliott wants his brother to be apart of his son's life, period. My presence in Grayson's life should have nothing to do with that and it would be fucked up of you to get in the way."

"Would it?"

I feel the button on my chill monitor break. This is not the woman I met a few weeks ago. She is not the same Tracy that sat at my dining room table crying and wishing us well in our future.

I retort, "You're such a bitch but guess what, I'm an even bigger one. I'm glad your dumb ass fucked up because I am going to enjoy prancing around in front of you with the man you lost on my arm. If you want to play those types of games, go ahead Tracy. You're wasting your time, I'm not going anywhere and Grayson will *never* be with you again."

She springs to her feet staring at me with such fury. If looks could kill I would be one dead ass bitch.

"I'm trying to be nice, Farah."

"Yeah, well you fucked that shit up from the moment you sat down and opened your mouth. If you want to get to know me, get to *know* me. Don't come in here dangling my man's nephew over my head like that is supposed to do some shit. I don't do well with threats, Tracy. Now I'm *trying* to be nice but you are really trying your fucking luck with me. So what I'm going to do is let my fiancé and his brother, the father of your son, know what the hell you came in here trying to do. I will let them handle it. You say you still have feelings for Grayson but you are steadily attempting to continuously destroy him. It's not going to work this time."

She moves as though she is trying to inch her way across my desk. I ease to my feet, ready. "You make the wrong move, pregnant or not, I will mop your skinny ass from wall to wall in this office. Play with me if you want to. Maybe Elliott should have let you know beforehand, I am *not* the one to play with. You can find some act right and we can start this conversation over or you can get the fuck out of my office. You decide."

Her voice cracks under her words as she says, "It's bad enough I had to witness it a few weeks ago but to constantly see him with you, I can't. I'm Jaime's mother and if I don't like you then you won't be around him. I have every bit of say so in *that*."

And I am Grayson's *wife*," I sneer. "This is a packaged deal, honey. Be a good mother and think about your child and the life you are holding him from by keeping him away from his family. And whether you like it or not, in two months I will be his family too. You're only hurting yourself and your son by acting this way. I have no beef with you and even after this horrible attempt at threatening me; I will still be woman enough to work with you for the sake of the man I love and his family. You will *never* be me Tracy and I mean that on *all* levels. I'm not going anywhere so you might as hang it up with a coat hanger."

I can tell by her expression that I have hit a nerve. She narrows her eyes at me, grabs her purse up in her arms forcefully and storms out. The room rattles from the might of the door slamming shut behind her. I am furious; my blood pressure is probably sky high. With a shaken hand, I hit the speed dial to call Grayson.

He answers on the second ring, "Good morning beautiful."

"Grayson...we have a problem."

| UNSTABLE REACTIONS

I could have been an extra in *Fast and Furious* as fast as I'm driving. I gun it through a red light, damn near pop a wheelie turning the corner, and Tokyo drift into the parking lot of Farah's job. I'm out of the car so fast, I have to double back and make sure I actually put the shit in park. My feet are moving quickly beneath me as I jog, damn near sprint up to the building. Noticing that I'm rushed, Jerry nods my way. I'm too impatient to wait on the elevator so I take the stairs up two at a time to the fifth floor. Breathless and furious all at once, I barrel into the lobby with a flushed face and sweat covered brow. Her receptionist Erin looks at me with wide eyes.

"Uh...good morning Mr. Powell, is everything okay?"

"Is Farah in her office?"

Her eyes move about feverishly, she doesn't know what to do any more than me.

I inhale sharply; try to stop my heart from racing. "I need to see her, it's important."

"Yes sir...she's...um...in her office."

I don't wait for her to give me the green light to go back before I'm racing down the hall to her office. She's barefoot, pacing the floors like her mind is gone bad. The curls that hung longingly before she left the house are now pushed up into a messy ponytail atop her head. She's in fighting stance, angry. She looks up at me through incensed grey eyes. An angry, pregnant woman is the scariest sight to see.

"You will not ever be around her if I'm not there, are we clear?"

Her tone makes the hairs on the back of my neck stand up.

"Farah, calm down."

"Calm down!" she exclaims. "That fucking bitch comes in here threatening me and you want me to calm down? You're lucky I didn't bash her damn face into this desk when I had the chance."

"Baby, you're going to yell the building down. Please lower your voice before you have everybody in our business."

"Fuck them," she spats. "I don't give a fuck who hears me right now."

"You're going to stress yourself into the hospital and I swear to God, if you put my daughter in danger I will never forgive you."

Though anger is still thumping through her veins, her eyes begin to soften and I can see the tears welding up.

"You don't mean that," she stammers.

Now that I'm sure the lioness has been tamed down to a kitten, I move over to where she's standing wrapping my arms around her. "I don't want anything happening to either of you so please calm down and lets talk about this."

"There's nothing to discuss," she says curtly pulling away from me. "I don't want you in her presence without me."

"Farah, I'm a grown ass man. I'm not about to sit here and debate this with you."

She narrows her eyes at me and I can't help but think she's the sexiest thing moving on this earth right now.

"Grayson Michael!"

"Farah Elise! I know you probably want to kick her ass...well no, I'm pretty sure you do...but I will handle it on my own. I don't need you doing any more than you already have. Just be my wife and be pregnant."

As much as she's trying to save face, I see a hint of a smile glimmer at the corners of her mouth.

"You're not so big and bad now," I tease pulling her in close to me, our lips just inches apart. "The whole office is probably wondering what the hell is going on."

She shrugs. "I don't care what they think. I'm going home, I need a drink."

My mouth falls into a flat line. "You better be talking about some damn water."

"Mm, nope...I'm going to pour myself the biggest glass of red wine I can find."

"The fuck you are."

She smirks. "My doctor said I could and after dealing with your pissy ass ex-girlfriend, *this* is not up for debate."

I can't fight her, I won't. I'm just happy she didn't do anything foolish, happy she and my daughter are in one piece. I press my lips to hers savoring the feel of her softness.

"I'll let you slide this time but next time I won't be so nice."

"Elliot, you better fix this shit! I swear!"

I glare at my brother cradling his head in his hands as he sits at his dining room table.

"Grayson, I had no idea she would do something like that."

"I trusted that by sitting down and talking to her things would be good, for *you*. I did that shit for you and your son and now she goes and tries to threaten my family."

He groans loudly. "She asked me for Farah's number talking about she wanted to talk to her, make arrangements for you and her to see Jaime. I told her no. If there was any meeting, I would set it up. She hasn't been right in years Grayson. It's like she's holding on to this small glimmer of hope that one day you will give her another chance."

"So what the fuck is you saying, this bitch is crazy?"

"Easy on the name calling, lets just say she's seeking help for some things."

"Nah see, no fucking way! Yes I feel better having gotten shit off of my chest but I'm done but I am not dealing with a damn Looney tune. She is trying to end up on *Snapped*! She knows where I live, goodness forbid she decides to pop up. This is too much."

I feel like Farah did earlier, pacing the floors like a mad man.

"You could have told me she was touched man."

He sighs. "She's been doing a lot better since she started taking medication. She's depressed Grayson; she's been through some shit in the last few years."

"I don't care!" I utter exasperated. "Is that supposed to make shit better?"

"No, nothing will make it better. No matter how you slice it, she was dead ass wrong. It will be fixed soon; I'm taking her to court for custody."

His words stop me in my tracks. I have to take a seat to gather myself. "Run that past me again."

"You heard me; I'm taking her for custody. She's been doing some ole crazy shit lately. I told her she has one more time to act out and we're going to see a judge about a little boy. This is the last straw. I don't feel comfortable with my son being fully in her care anymore especially so far away."

"When did all of this start?"

"A couple of months after you two broke up. She took the break up really hard and then a few months after that her father passed away. You know how close they were. It was like her on/off switch broke the fuck off and she's been off ever since. One weekend she came up here babbling about wanting to be with you and then another weekend she comes up here *without* Jamie trying to throw herself at me. I was giving her the benefit of the doubt but when she starts fucking with Farah,

I can't let that slide. I already contacted a lawyer and we're going to meet later this week to get the paperwork together."

The thought makes my stomach turn but I ask anyway, "Do you think she would hurt Farah?"

He glowers over at me as if offended that I would ask such a thing. "No Grayson, I don't think she's *that* out of touch. I mean, if she was going to physically hurt her she would have had the perfect opportunity today. I know that's harsh but it's the truth. I have been trying to talk her into handing over custody so she can go seek professional help but she's not hearing it. I have no other choice but to do this shit the hard way."

I'm thoroughly disgusted by all that has been revealed to me. I stagger to my feet; my head is somewhere up in the clouds. "I'm going to get out of here."

Elliott replies, "This is our child and my mess. Don't tell Farah. I don't want her to be shaken up or anything."

"Farah? Shaken up? Ha, that's the last thing she is but I won't say anything to her."

The smell of dinner is still lingering in the air. It is well after eleven when I step into the house, tiptoeing. After the talk Elliott and I had, somehow I made a detour to a bar a few minutes from the house. I intended to have one beer which turned into three and six shots. Needless to say, drunkenness is settling in. I manage to make it up the steps without creating a ruckus. The light from the television seeps through the crack of our jarred bedroom door. I mentally cuss myself at the sight of

Farah sitting up in bed staring aimlessly at the television screen. The volume is barely above mute. God only knows how long she has been sitting here like this.

"Where have you been?" she says through gritted teeth.

I feel like a deer caught in headlights. No matter what I say, she's pissed and this is not going to be a pretty conversation.

"I stopped to see Elliott on the way home from work."

"That's where you've been for the last few hours?" she asks flatly.

"No," I answer. "I stopped at the bar for a few drinks. It's been a bit of a rocky day."

She runs a frustrated hand through her hair. "Let me get this straight: you stay out until damn near midnight and didn't even bother to call and tell me shit? I have been calling you back-to-back for the last three hours, worried *sick* and your ass is at some fucking bar throwing back drinks. Thank you for your damn consideration, Grayson! Anything could have happened."

I feel like a child being reprimanded by his mother. I was in the wrong and I can't do anything else but take the verbal beating.

"I know," I mutter. "My phone died. I'm sorry."

"I had a shitty day too or have you forgotten. I was really looking forward to you coming home, having dinner ready when you got here. I was going to run you a bath and fuck your damn brains out but no, your punk ass is just now strolling in like everything is honky dory!"

Damn it, I missed all of that!

I totter over to the bed. The room is beginning to spin and if I don't sit down, I'm going to spin my ass into the floor.

"Ugh! You smell like liquor."

Wounded by her words, I stammer. "I'll sleep on the floor."

She says nothing, simply rolls over and covers her body with the comforter. For the next thirty minutes, I stare blankly at the blurred figures on the television. Her soft snores let me know she is finally sleeping. With great urge, I amble off unsteadily to the bathroom to have a talk with the porcelain god.

| FORGIVENESS

I lie in bed wide awake staring at the wall. The little girl inside of me is jumping around like she is in a bounce house. Suddenly, I feel sick to my stomach. I gather myself enough to sit up. It takes everything I can manage to pull myself to my feet and move in the direction of the bathroom.

"Holy shit," I holler at the sight of Grayson sprawled out on the bathroom floor.

Luckily, there's a straight path to the toilet. Within seconds I am doubled over throwing up last night's dinner. Amidst my unpleasant deposit of puke into the toilet, I hear Grayson moan as he stirs in the floor at my feet.

Sleepily, he asks, "Farah...baby, are you okay?"

I roll my eyes; hit the lever on the toilet to flush it before making my way to the sink to brush my teeth.

"I'm fine," I say curtly.

I watch him stumble to his feet in the mirror as I brush. He is so handsome, so mine and I hate that I can't be mad at him but for a second. I examine his face. He needs to shave though the scruff look is working in his favor right about now. He perches himself on the edge of the tub watching me as I watch him in the mirror.

"I'm sorry," he says, his eyes full of remorse.

I swish water around in my mouth a few times until traces of the toothpaste are gone and my mouth feels clean again.

I turn to face him, tell him, "Apology accepted."

"Can I have a hug?"

When I fall into his arms, I find my comfort and security in them. I settle myself into his lap securing my arms around his neck.

"I promise I won't do that again."

"I told you, apology accepted. Lets just move on from it, ok."

"Sure."

I crinkle my nose at him. "Grayson, you stink."

He pushes me up on my feet so I am standing between his legs. Slowly, he eases my panties down over my hips and thighs into the floor. My eyes are stuck on him, a burning pleasure ignies from deep within.

"Shower with me," he says in a husky tone.

Oh this man!

And I can't say no, not that I want to anyway. "Okay...I'll start the shower while you brush your teeth."

He laughs heartily and everything in the world is right again.

"Don't ask," I insist shuffling past Cathy in the hallway on the way to my office.

She's not hearing it as she turns abruptly, fast on my heels. "Oh the hell I will. You have some explaining to do."

She shuts the door behind us blocking out intruding ears. "Now I let you slide yesterday but you better start talking," she says taking a seat, her arms crossed over her chest in a motherly stance.

I give in; tell her the Spark notes version without delving too deep. Her eyes bug, her mouth is wide open as if I just told her the most amazing story ever. By the end, my head is pounding and I want one mean cup of coffee.

"And you're about to marry this man with all of his craziness."

I shake my head. "I know and I love him to death."

"That's the hard part about love. You can't help who you fall in love with and you can't help everything that comes along with them. You can either love them enough to deal with it or love them enough to move on so you don't hurt them any further."

For the first time in the last twenty four hours, I cry. I feel broken and I have no understanding as to why. Cathy races around my desk throwing her arms around me.

"Ok, no...please don't cry. I can't stand to see you crying."

"I'm sorry. Damn these hormones!"

I use the tissues she hands me from the box sitting on my desk to dab at my eyes. Once I have gotten my emotional ass under control, I stand to my feet grabbing my briefcase.

"I'm going to spend the rest of the week out of the office."

"I think that's best. You don't have any clients today but I will make sure to switch things around for you for the rest of the week. Go home and rest, for the sake of you and the baby."

I feel the tears resurfacing as I scoop her up into another hug. "I swear you are the best. I love you; I will be in touch later on today."

Twenty minutes later, I am walking through the double doors of Grayson's office. The secretary, Thomas, gives me a toothy smile.

"Good morning, Ms. Acosta...I mean, Mrs. Powell."

I chuckle at his confusion. "Good morning Thomas. It's still Ms. Acosta. Is Grayson available by chance?"

"I'll page him and let him know you are here."

"Thank you."

He picks up the receiver, punches in his extension, and says, "Mr. Powell, Ms. Acosta is here to see you."

I expect him to tell me I can proceed to his office. Before such words can even form to leave his mouth, Grayson flies around the corner. He rushes up to me, cups my face in his hands searching it frantically. "Farah, are you okay?"

"I'm fine. I just wanted to see you."

Wordlessly, he grabs my hand pulling me back to his office. Once in the confinements of his four walls, I lose myself in his arms.

"You're scaring me," he says after awhile. "Are you sure you're okay."

"I promise. I just wanted to feel your arms around me."

He tightens his hold around my frame. "How is this?"

"Better...much better."

I BEFORE THE ALTAR

Life has slowly crept back to some sort of normalcy within the last two months. And when I open my eyes on this Friday morning, I can't help but feel overcome with happiness at the thought of marrying the woman beside me tomorrow. I watch her sleep peacefully for a moment. In a few hours, her mother and sister are going to steal her away from me and we will be apart until we reunite at the altar. She is heaven sent, flawless lying naked beneath our sheets. I move in close to her planting kisses at the corners of her mouth. She stirs beneath my lips, her eyes flutter open sleepily.

"I couldn't help myself." I explain immediately as if answering the question I see written across her face.

She stretches then stirs snuggling up into my arms. Even though she is fresh out of sleep, her morning breath is tolerable as she captures my lips with hers. Her belly hinders the space between us but she is close enough for me to feel the warmth blistering between her legs. Her breasts are full and swelling beneath my hand as I massage one gently running her protruding nipple under my fingertip. She groans from the heightening pleasure that resounds through her body. I can barely contain my anxious erection as I rest up on my knees turning her over on her side. I sink deep inside of her, her warmth and undue wetness sends me reeling. I clench my eyes shut, try to shift my thoughts to something else to take the focus off of how good she feels in this moment. She meets me thrust for thrust whirling her hips around me welcoming me further inside. I feel her body tense, her fingernails dig into my arm and she climaxes around me in the sweetest array of purrs and moans. And right on cue, I pour into her like an empty cup.

"So this is how Grayson Powell is living?"

Shaun Gonzalez stands in the middle of the living room looking around like it's a tourist attraction. Jeffrey Lewis steps in behind him shaking his head with sanction, says, "Bro, this shit dope!"

I have known Shaun and Jeffrey for years, old college football buddies that I haven't seen in ages but stay in constant contact with. Shaun lives in Texas with his wife and son while Jeffrey is living in Detroit still basking in his bachelor ways.

Farah clears her throat drawing our attention to where she is standing in the doorway, a small duffle bag resting on her shoulder.

"Gentleman…"

Jeffrey is first to greet her with a hug. "It's a pleasure to finally meet you after all these years of his and byes over the phone."

She laughs. "Yes…finally. It's good to meet you."

Shaun swoops in to hug her next, a light one as not to suffocate her with his overbearing weight. "You look great, Farah. How are things?"

"Things are wonderful. How are the wife and son?"

"They are doing well, keeping me on my toes."

Her eyes settle on me and I can't help but to smile at my prize.

"I'm about to leave," she tells me. "Mami is outside."

"I'll be right back fellas," I say following her out to the front door.

She drops the bag at her feet, wraps her arms around my waist pulling me in close to her; she looks up at me, says, "Don't you get too crazy tonight."

I smile down at her; run my index finger down the side of her face pushing strands of hair back behind her ear. "What is your definition of crazy?"

She frowns. "Grayson Powell, don't play with me."

I bring my hand up to the nape of her neck running my fingers through the curls of hair that rest there. I hold her head steady so she can't wrestle away from the kiss I plant on her lips.

"Lets defy tradition and spend tonight together."

"And have to hear that lady outside bitch about driving twenty minutes here to pick me up," she replies with her lips still pressed against mine.

I pull away from her, sure that if I don't I'm going to want to take her upstairs and do things to her that will have our houseguests sick of hearing my name. And when I see that devious smirk on her face, I know she is thinking the same thing.

"If you don't get going, you're going to hear it either way."

I bend to grab the bag but she slaps my hand away, utters, "I'm not helpless baby, I can carry it."

Just as round and pregnant as can be, she thinks she is superwoman never wanting anyone to do too much for her that she swears she can do on her own. I say nothing; just watch her bend at the knees to grab the handle of the bag before swinging it up and over her shoulder again.

"I'll call you before it gets too late..."

She shakes her head. The same strands I pushed away a few moments ago fall back in her face. "No you won't. You're going to enjoy this time with your friends, get drunk for the *both* of us, and go see naked bitches swing on poles or whatever trouble you have planned for the night."

I chortle fully.

"I just want you to have fun and cling to your last hours of being a single-before-married man."

Like a puppy dog, I poke my lip out and furrow my brow. "Not even a text message?"

She rolls her eyes with a giggle. "Fine, *one* text message. I mean it, go have fun."

Her mother beeps the horn twice more, impatiently. I run my hands along her belly feeling my daughter cradle against the warmth of my hand. "I love you…I love my girls."

"We love you too."

She takes a handful of my shirt in her grip pulling me down in a passionate kiss. I push my tongue into the comfort of her mouth savoring the taste of her.

"You better go before that woman comes in here after you," I pant carting away from her.

"I will see you at the altar, Mr. Powell," she states with a wink.

I watch her turn and open the door. She looks over her shoulder at me, blows me a kiss.

"I'll be waiting."

| Bells Will Be Ringing

"I'm not going out there. I look like a blimp in curtains and frills."

Unashamed, my sister cocks her head back and laughs. I mean laughs like I am a stand up comedian and I just told the funniest joke she ever heard, laughs so hard her eyes water.

"Bitch this shit isn't funny! I'm not walking down the aisle looking like this."

Mami stifles a snicker with her hand. "Farah, cut it out. You are a beautiful *pregnant* woman and you will go out there and marry that man come hell or hot water. If I have to call him to come get you my damn self, I will do it."

I'm so nervous I can't tell if there are butterflies in my stomach or my baby girl doing the electric slide right now. Tears threaten my eyes with much success.

"Oh my goodness Farah, you don't have to cry about it."

Mami narrows her eyes at Clarissa. "Nobody said anything to you when you were crying in the middle of the supermarket because nobody would buy you a tub of ice cream when you were pregnant. Go get me a damn tissue girl."

Clarissa slinks away down the hall to do as she is told.

I wipe tears away with the back of my hand catching them before they can dissolve into the fabric of my dress. Clarissa reappears shoving a handful of tissues into my palm. I dab at my cheeks, turn back to the mirror to access myself once more. I am dressed in a soft ivory colored chiffon gown with a lace appliqué and a sweep train. The fabric falls flowingly over my baby bump, my breasts pushed up perfectly in the bodice. My hair is swept up into a pin curled up-do creating a completed look of elegance.

"You look stunning Farah," Clarissa says softly coming up behind me, our eyes fixed on each other's in the mirror. "Grayson is going to love you regardless of the dress you have on."

I smile nervously.

"I'm a wreck," I admit.

"But you're a beautiful one. Come on so we can get your makeup done and get you to the church to marry your man."

I plop down in front of the vanity mirror in mami and papa's master bathroom. I watch as Clarissa transforms my face with gold, brown, and bronze eye shadows, nude lipstick, and natural foundations and blush across my cheeks. It reminds me of the makeup she used to paint me perfect on my first date with Grayson. I feel tears pricking at my eyes. Forcefully, I hold back the urge. I have to say I look amazing, glowing brighter than I ever have before. This is one of the biggest days of my life, a day I never thought I would actually experience at the rate I was going.

The ride to the church seems to stretch on forever. At one point, I felt like asking the driver if we were there yet but the stern expression plastered on his face made me change my mind. Like thieves in the night, we manage to make it inside of the vestibule unseen. As quickly as I can manage in my ivory Jessica Simpson pumps, I shuffle down the corridor to the designated room for myself and my bridal party.

I wish I could have a damn shot of something right now, I think wearing the carpet thin under my feet as I pace to and from.

The knock at the door scares me so bad, I damn near piss myself. Papa eases inside of the room looking debonair in his black tuxedo accentuated with a rich cream color.

"Aw baby girl, you look stunning."

I quickly turn my back to him; take a few deep breaths, say, "papa please, I'm trying not to cry."

"I'm sorry baby girl; I just came to let you know most of the guests are here. Whenever you're ready, we can start."

"Go Anthony," I hear mami say through gritted teeth. "She's going to ruin her makeup with you in here."

Terri steps in front of me, rests her hands on my shoulders. She looks amazing in the purple bridesmaid dress I picked for her.

"At this rate, you're going to break before you even make it down the aisle. Take a deep breath and relax a little bit, girl."

My mouth feels like I've been shuffling cotton balls from cheek to cheek.

"I know," I stammer swallowing hard. "I'm ready. I just want to say I do and get this over with."

I stand stock still while mami places my veil over my hair and Clarissa makes finishing touches to my makeup. All eyes are on me, waiting for my signal. I inhale sharply taking in another deep breath before shaking my head to go ahead and open the door. The sound of heels clicking against the marble floors as we walk down the elongated hallway force my thoughts back to memories of my first time meeting Grayson. I think back to the Dominican Republic, the many nights of making love, the tears, the arguments, all of the good and bad things that have led up to this moment. My hands are sweating, I'm gripping the handle of my bouquet as if it is about to run away from me. I see papa and he is waiting on me, smiling at me proudly. When I reach the end of the hallway, I link my arm through his allowing him to escort me to the double doors leading into the sanctuary. I inhale his familiar scent. He has been wearing the same fragrance for years. I don't know the name but it is a smell that is only his and it brings me much comfort each and every time. Anxiously, we stand watching the flower girl, ring bearer, bridesmaids and groomsmen, and lastly mami make their way down the carpeted aisle. India

Arie's *Beautiful Surprise* begins to play. Papa reaches over and pats my hand comfortingly. I look over at him and him at me, smile just as the oak doors open up.

For a split second my heart stops, my breath catches in my throat. Our eyes lock and my feet feel like boulders, unable to move. He is so handsome, so perfect standing there at the altar in his black and cream tailcoat tuxedo. I watch him sniffle, reach up and wipe tears away with the support of his hand. I am stuck on stupid or love or whatever it is that won't allow me to move any further. Papa tugs on my arm coaxing me forward. Blissful eyes stare at me, watching and waiting. And slowly, ever so slowly I take my first steps toward my future.

Somewhere between the exchanging of vows and being pronounced husband and wife, I come down off of my little cloud just in time to kiss Grayson for our first moment as a married couple. Applause erupts throughout the church, cameras flash all around us and the whole time we are in our own little world. He kisses me fully, clinging to me as if his legs aren't enough to support his weight. In these single seconds, he has transformed into another man—my man, my *husband* and I am so in love.

| WRITTEN GOODBYES

I turn my truck into our driveway, park next to Farah's Nissan that has been sitting in the same spot for the last three days. It's a Tuesday morning, the perfect degree of not too hot and not too cold. I have spent the last two nights and one day cooped up in a hotel suite with Farah making love and enjoying blissful moments as husband and wife. Farah is in the passenger's seat with her mouth hung open and her head cocked to one side snoring softly. Though the drive home lasted all of thirty minutes, I conclude she must be spent from the late nights and early morning. I lean over and kiss the spot underneath her earlobe. Stirring awake, a moan escapes her as her eyes open.

"We're home sleepy head."

She rolls her neck a few times wiping the corners of her mouth where drool had begun to form. She yawns loudly gathering her belongings before climbing out of the car. I retrieve our bags from the trunk as she fumbles for the house keys in her purse.

"I would carry you over the threshold but the way my back is set up…"

She chuckles turning the key in the lock, pushing the front door open. "I wouldn't expect you to body all of this weight but thank you."

The house is the way I left it and immediately I remember the mess I left in the living room. Luckily, she makes a beeline for the stairs avoiding the trip down the hall.

"I'm sleepy," she says slowly climbing the steps. "I'm going back to bed."

"I'm going to check some emails and make some calls; I'll check on you in a little while."

She mumbles something but she is too far up the steps for me to comprehend her words.

I dispose of the beer bottles and paper plates I left strewn around the living room from our guy's night in a garbage bag. I straighten the throw pillows on the couch before settling behind the desk in my office. I have no missed calls but there are a dozen missed emails that require my response. I sigh heavily opening the most recent one. Judging by the length and verbiage, I know I'm going to be here for awhile and I am not the least bit enthused.

I don't realize I have fallen asleep until I awaken to the sound of the doorbell ringing repeatedly and Farah yelling down the hall at me, "What the fuck, Grayson! You don't hear the doorbell?"

It is well after three o' clock I find from the digital numbers on the bottom right hand side of the computer screen.

"Damn it; knock me over why don't you!"

I hear Elliott say sternly, "Is my brother here?"

I make it into the living room before Elliott can make it to the office, his eyes wide and face wan. He looks disheveled like he has just fought off a gang of people.

"Whoa! Slow down, what's up?" I ask.

He sputters, "We need to talk...in private."

Farah is standing a few feet behind him with her arms crossed over her belly, her hair still in disarray from her nap.

My eyes shift to her then back to him, I ask, "Is this something she will need to know?"

He exhales exasperated. "Yes...eventually. Grayson please, we need to talk *now*."

I turn to lead him into the office. "Come on."

Over my shoulder I hear Farah suck her teeth and stomp off down the hall. I know I will have to hear it later but right now my brother needs me. Once behind the closed door, he tosses a crinkled letter on the desk.

"Read it," he demands.

I stare at it for a few moments; a sinking feeling begins to form in the pit of my stomach.

"Who is this from?"

Agitated by the torrent of questions, he says, "Read the fucking letter Grayson. Damn...*please!*"

I work the letter open and begin to read:

Dear Elliott,

It's over. All of the anguish I have caused you and your family will be no more. I decided to turn over full custody of Jaime to you. We both know I am not mentally well and fully incapable of raising that little boy full-time. This is the last thing you will ever hear from me, the last words to ever be associated with me. By the time you get this, I will have gone on to another place. One far better than this one where I can cause no harm to you, your family, or anyone else. I love you and you have been a great friend to me, a wonderful father. Tell my son that I love him and when he gets older, explain to him the decisions I've made and why. Kiss him and hug him for me and make sure he is always loved. Please tell Grayson that no matter what has happened between us, I love him so much and I wish we could have worked out. Tell Farah, I'm sorry for the trouble I caused that day in her office. I hadn't taken my medication; I wasn't in my right mind. When you get this letter, please contact my mother at (302) 746-

8801. I left Jaime with her. So I guess this is it, all I had left to say.
You are a good man Elliott and you make sure the next woman to
come into your life is a much better mother than I ever was.

Love you always,

Tracy

P.S. – If by the time you get this, my mother has not found me,
call the police to my apartment.

I sit frozen, my eyes reading the last line over and over
again. I look at Elliott now sitting with his head in his hands
crying. Words have failed me completely. I'm not sure I fully
understand what I just read.

Before I can run scenarios around in my head, Elliott utters,
"By the time I called her mother, she was already *dead*. She
took all types of medications before cutting her wrists.
I...I...just didn't think she would ever kill herself."

He chokes on a sob and still I am stuck in my seat. I stare
perplexedly at him while he mourns, emotionless. My attention
is jarred when the door flies open. Farah is standing on the
other side, her face laced with concern.

"I heard crying," she explains rushing over to Elliott.

I can't lie and say I'm not thankful for her presence, her
gestures of sympathy when I am unable to produce any.

She rubs his back soothingly, her voice is pillow soft.
"Elliott, what's the matter?"

Her eyes search my face for answers. There are none, at
least none that I can provide at this minute. He says nothing
but somehow her touch, her presence has brought his sobs

down to whimpers. She pulls the empty chair up close to his, her face cringes from the pain in her back.

"It's probably none of my business," she tells him. "But I couldn't bear to hear you crying. What's wrong, Elliott?"

Again her eyes settle on me with question. When she doesn't get an answer, she huffs loudly in irritation. She waits, patiently, for him to speak. All at once, my mouth moves along with my legs.

"Tracy is dead," I reply.

My tone holds no compassion. Not purposely. It's a response that had not checked in with my brain before coming out.

"What?" she stammers.

I hand her the letter to read. I watch her as her eyes move feverishly across the paper. A hand clasps over her mouth as tears fall helplessly from her eyes. I accuse it to her pregnant hormones. She has no reason to cry for the woman that waltzed into her office threatening her just weeks before.

"I am so sorry Elliott."

He wipes his face with the back of his hands and palms. His nose is reddening along with his eyes. I walk around the front of the desk and put a comforting arm around him.

"We will help you get through this," I say.

I'm not convinced of my words. Helping my brother mourn the death of *my* ex-girlfriend, the mother of *his* child, is so ass backwards. My thoughts travel to Jaime, a little boy thrust into a fucked up situation made by his own parents. In just a letter with a stamp on it, his mother is gone from his life. No warning, no real goodbye just dropped off to his grandmother as if everything is normal. And now Elliott is a single father. Though it is what he wanted, it shouldn't have to come at this price. It reminds me of my own family and how they selfishly gave me and Elliott away; having to adjust to a new life, a new family. I know it all too well and my heart aches for the little boy sitting at his grandmother's house probably playing with his toys unaware that his mother is gone from this earth. I put my selfishness, my prideful thoughts to the side and console my brother through his devastating time.

I STUCK IN THE MIDDLE

For more than an hour, I sit through the stories of Tracy's troubled behaviors. How sick she was and how hidden they kept it, how she refused to seek help, and everything dealing with the custody battle that led to her wanting to end her own life. As I sit dabbing at my tear stained cheeks, I can't for the life of me comprehend why there is even a tear for me to shed. I didn't know her. Hell, a few weeks ago I was telling her how much I didn't like her and vindictively would enjoy showboating Grayson around in her presence. I immediately feel bad even when I was justified in how I felt at the time. I fix a meal of fried fish, fresh mashed potatoes, and salad. I try to get Elliott to eat something but he refuses. He prefers to drown his sorrows in brown liquors Grayson escaped to the store to buy. Every now and again his phone rings and he slinks off into the next room to take it. Later we find out it is Tracy's mother keeping him updated on everything. He plans to leave sometime tomorrow to go to Delaware to make the funeral arrangements and pack up Jaime's belongings. To think of him having to go to the very place she ended her life makes my soul cry out for him. I can only imagine. By the time ten o'clock rolls around, he's knocked out in a drunken induced sleep on the sofa bed. I'm thankful; the emotional rollercoaster has ended for the night.

Then there is Grayson who hasn't said much of anything for the past few hours. I'm sure this is all uncomfortable for him being that it was once his ex-girlfriend. I can't even measure how he must feel or even what is going through his mind. He won't talk let alone look at me for long. I busy myself with cleaning the kitchen up after dinner. I take extra care with washing the dishes instead of using the dishwasher the way I usually do. By the time I climb the steps to our bedroom, Grayson is already underneath the covers with his back turned toward the door. Knowing my husband the way I do, I am sure he is not sleep. His thoughts are probably running laps around his head. I tip toe into the bathroom to take a long, hot shower letting the water cascade down over my body.

We haven't been married for a full week and already some shit has happened, I think.

For the first time ever I wonder why Grayson's life couldn't be normal but then that wouldn't make him the man I know and love. After my shower I moisturize my skin with a Shea butter and vanilla lotion, tie my hair up high on my head, and slip into one of Grayson's oversized t-shirts. As I predicted, he is fully awake, his eyes piercing into mine as we lay facing one another.

"Tell me what you're thinking," I insist.

"I don't want to have to think about any of it. This is just way too much to deal with."

I frown. "You're not a victim here. Despite your past with her, your brother lost a friend...the mother of his child."

He huffs rolling over on his back. "I'm not playing a victim. I don't know how to react, how to deal with any of it. She's like a stranger to me now and I have no emotions about it but I know my brother needs me."

"And that's just it, he needs you."

"You don't get it."

"Obviously, I don't," I say sourly. I turn over like a fish out of water to face the window.

After a moment, I feel the bed move and his body heat blankets over me as he rests his hand on my stomach.

"Don't be angry with me. I really don't know how to channel my feelings right now."

"I can tell," I reply softly. "Elliott knows too but he needs our support. It's not about Tracy, Grayson. It's about his son and the fact that he is going to be a single father from now on. There are no visitations, no calls from her...she is gone. He needs us to help him and that is all I am trying to get you to understand. I'm not asking you to shed a tear for the girl, I'm just asking you to have some sympathy toward your brother's situation."

He exhales. His warm breath whispers against the back of my neck.

"I can do that."

"Thank you."

"Are you sure you aren't mad at me?" he asks.

I smile even when I was trying my best not to. "Yes, I'm sure. I'm just tired from today's event, that's all."

He presses his lips to the back of my ear, trailing kisses down to my shoulder blade. "How tired is tired?"

His hand travels down between my thighs cupping my sex in his palm. My insides ignite and I immediately become a slave to his touch.

I am up early, seven o'clock to be exact according to the alarm clock by the bed. It's not that I am well rested but rather that I am hot as shit with Grayson clinging to me like wet clothes. I feel myself sweating, damn near suffocating. I wrestle from underneath the weight of his arm. My t-shirt, technically his, is dampened with perspiration. I fight my way out of bed; my leg is imprisoned by the bed sheet. I brush my teeth, change my shirt, and slide on a pair of sweatpants before going downstairs. After peeking into the living room, I see that the other man in my house is still deep in his sleep. I busy myself in the kitchen as if I hadn't just left out of here a few hours before.

Hell, I'm the pregnant one. Why isn't anyone cooking for me?

On second thoughts, I'm kind of glad to have the distraction. I have one more day off and I at least hope I can salvage some of today for relaxation purposes. I open the *Pandora* application on my phone, set it in the cradle of the speaker system and let Elle Varner sing to me while I dance around the kitchen. Some bacon here, a few eggs there, and a couple of golden brown pancakes top the serving dishes I've placed on the counter.

"You move well for a pregnant woman."

Elliott is standing in the doorway of the kitchen rubbing his temples, his eyes squinting against the brightness in the room.

"I can cut a rug," I joke. "Don't let this baby fool you."

Without him asking, I make my way over to the cupboard that houses the Tylenol and first aid kit. I fill a glass with water, shake two pills from the bottle and hand them to him.

He gives me a tired smile. I know it well and it is not the kind of tired that can be cured by sleep. It is that emotional tired that drains you from the inside out.

"Thank you."

He takes a seat on one of the stools overlooking the island countertop. In one swift move he pops the pills into his mouth and washes them down with a few gulps of water.

"I guess my brother is still sleep," he says.

"Last I checked."

"How is he?"

The question catches me off guard. Guilty is the man that cares more for the thoughts and concerns of his brother rather than the depths of his own sorrow.

"That doesn't really matter, how are you?"

"I'm as good as I'm going to get," he replies. "I'm still trying to take it all in, you know."

I nod with understanding.

"You're a strong woman," he tells me. "You have handled everything so well when most others would have faltered by now."

"This isn't a job. This is the life of the man I love which has now become my own. The only reward I seek is the happiness of me and those around me. I don't give up on people I love."

"I wish I had a woman that won't give up on me." His tone is melancholy, regretful.

"Eventually you will but right now you have a little boy that needs your full attention. I am a firm believer that all things happen for a reason. Be patient Elliott, things take place when they are supposed to."

Before he can speak, a yawning Grayson comes bounding into the room. His pajama pants hang from his hips, his penis resting scrumptiously against his thigh.

"Good morning."

I look over at Elliott and smile comfortingly then at my husband.

"Good morning baby, you're just in time for breakfast."

We sit at the kitchen table to eat and it is as awkward as the day is long. My appetite is lost and I find myself looking at them as they devour everything on their plates.

"You haven't eaten much of anything," Grayson says pointing out the obvious.

"I thought I was hungry but I'm not."

He furrows his eyebrow. "You need to eat though, there's a baby that needs to eat."

It's more a reprimand than a concern.

"Elliott, can I get you anything else?" I ask in an attempt to create a diversion.

I feel his eyes burning into me. My lack of sleep has finally caught up to me and I have no energy to argue.

Nervously, Elliott replies, "No, I'm okay."

"I mean it Farah, you can't ignore me. You need to eat."

I cut my eyes at him. "When I am hungry, I *will* eat. I'm not hungry right now."

Elliott swallows back the last of his orange juice, stands to his feet. "I need to go so I can get home and pack before I hit the road."

"I will walk you out," he retorts. Though he is talking to his brother, his stare is fixed on me.

Elliott bends to hug me, placing a firm hand on my stomach.

He leans in and whispers, "I hate seeing you two argue, just try to eat for him ok."

"Okay," I say.

I avoid eye contact with Grayson as they walk out. I hate his mannish ways sometimes. Just because I don't eat right this minute doesn't mean my child is at jeopardy. I let out a frustrated groan as I stuff a piece of bacon into my mouth. It's cold and it takes all I can muster to swallow it down and take another bite. Grayson returns just as I take a bite of a pancake. Despite the frown on my face, he looks pleased. Whole time, I am two seconds away from spitting this shit back in the plate.

"Thank you for eating."

"I'm only doing it because your brother asked me to. I told you I wasn't hungry."

He shakes his head discontented, says nothing as he stands back to his feet and exits stage left. I grab a napkin out of the holder and spit the chewed up food into it. With a roll of my eyes, I push to my feet to clean up the dirty dishes.

I can't wait to have this little girl!

| CLOSING CHAPTERS

For the next two days, I stay locked up in my office fronting like I am doing work when really I am unfocused and accomplishing next to nothing.

"The funeral will be next Thursday morning and the wake is Wednesday night here in Delaware," Elliott tells me Friday afternoon.

Tracy didn't have much saved up and her mother is struggling just the same leaving the expense of the funeral in his lap. He graciously agreed to pay for everything. In my mind I think he's crazy but I don't tell him that.

"Even if you don't come to the actual funeral, I would appreciate it if you came down to help me with Jaime's stuff."

Of course I wouldn't go to her damn funeral!

"Yeah sure, I can do that."

"Thank you. I need to go but I just wanted to keep you updated."

"I appreciate it, you be safe."

"Will do, see you next week."

I refocus, or at least attempt to, my attention back to the email I have been trying to compose for the last hour. There are several new projects on the table for the firm and I have a shitload of emails to respond to. Unfortunately, my brain has stopped working and words that would normally come easy haven't come at all. Frustrated by my inability to work, I grab a bottle of brandy off of the mini bar and a glass to pour it in.

Fuck it, I think taking the drink to the head.

It's happy hour somewhere in this world.

"Are you going to go to the funeral?"

Shadows of light illuminate Farah's face as she looks over at me. Up until now, the ride to Delaware has been a quiet one. Traffic is rather light for a Wednesday evening. The smooth drive put Farah to sleep before we even got through the first toll. Now she is up, an hour later, and wanting to talk.

"No Farah, I'm not going. Are you?"

She purses her lips at me as if she deserved a better answer to her dumb ass question.

"No," she replies. "I didn't know her like that and she wasn't exactly fond of me."

"So what makes you think I would want to go to her damn funeral?"

She grows silent, fidgets in her seat. "Because you once loved her...I don't know."

I chuckle at the audacity of her question. "Farah, just stop talking please. What you are asking is asinine!"

"I'm sorry." Her voice is low, shaken.

I don't have time for this crying shit, I tell myself. *Please not right now.*

"I *once* loved her, yes but I don't anymore. Honestly, how many times do you want to hear me say that? You know how I felt about her. Why would you think I would want to be at her funeral?"

"I wasn't thinking. I'm sorry; this is all still very weird to me."

"I think she might turn over in her casket if we walked through the door anyway," I say lightly.

"Grayson, that's not nice."

Despite her words, she can't hide her hilarity.

She diverts her attention to the lit up stores along the highway as we drive past. I reach over and palm her stomach.

"We don't have a name for her yet," I say.

"It's been so much going on lately, you know."

"We have time now, lets do it."

I can't see it but I hear the smile in her voice.

"Okay, any suggestions."

"What do you think about Nicole?"

She turns her face up at the idea. "That's mami's middle name."

"I know."

She giggles. "She would probably do back flips in the hospital if we did that but no, what else."

"Um...what about Nia?"

"I like Nia. Nia...Renee...Nia Renee Powell, what do you think?"

She moves suddenly beneath my hand. "I think she likes it. I like it too."

Farah cringes in pain. "She just kicked the shit out of me; I'll say she likes it."

I can't help but laugh though Farah is nothing close to amused. We spend the rest of the ride talking about arrangements for the arrival of baby Nia. And for the first time in days, I am laughing and smiling again.

We spend Thursday driving around like two awestruck tourists taking advantage of the tax-free shopping at *Christiana Mall*, visiting the *Museum of Natural History*, and dining out at an authentic Italian pizzeria with the large slices that grease through the bag. By nightfall we elect to stay in the hotel and order Chinese food from a restaurant a few minutes away while we watch television. And now here it is Friday morning, seven o'clock according to my phone as it rings displaying Elliott's name on the ID.

"Good morning, sorry if I woke you."

"No, it's fine," I grumble.

He pauses to address someone talking to him in the background. "Yeah, sorry about that...do you think you can be here by nine?"

Farah is beginning to stir awake, her eyes slowly easing open.

"Sure, nine is fine. Send me the address and we will be there."

In the time that Tracy and I dated, I met her parents on two separate occasions and both times was when they visited the DC area. This is new to me, I am in foreign territory. The address leads us to a rundown neighborhood about twenty minutes away. The narrow street her mother lives on is lined with terraced style homes. Their front yards are no bigger than a minute with one car garages. The house is tucked away in a corner. There are Christmas lights still hanging from the outside windows and around the door. I pull up behind Elliott's car and park. I take a deep breath and exhale loudly. I haven't seen this woman in years and it is not actually a blissful occasion as a reason to be seeing her again. Farah reaches over and squeezes my hand. She says nothing but that special gesture alone speaks volumes to me. I lean over and kiss her fully. She smiles at me and I suddenly don't feel as nervous anymore. After helping Farah out of the car, we walk up to the front door hand-in-hand. Before I can put my finger to the doorbell, the front door flies open and Mrs. Peters is on the other side.

"Hi Grayson."

She has aged and not in a good way. It is evident her black has cracked, completely. She has gained several unflattering pounds around the midsection; her hair is now thinning and grey. Her eyes have sunken in, darkened with large bags under each one.

"Hello Mrs. Peters," I stammer.

"Come on in," she says stepping back to let us through.

The inside is a mirror of the outside, small. The hallway is constricted; no two people can stand side by side comfortably. The faint smell of cigarette smoke lingers in the air but I don't recall her ever being a smoker. She leads us into the living room where Elliott is throwing toys into a cardboard box.

"Hey, I was wondering where you two were."

"There was some traffic," I reply.

The living room is a closet with a small couch and a loveseat. The walls are an ugly color brown with gaudy wallpaper around the top. It seems crowded but I can't tell if it's the coffee table or the entertainment system that's taking up the majority of the space.

"You must be Farah," Mrs. Peters states giving her a once over. She eyes her stomach and even I feel the discomfort behind her gaze.

"Yes ma'am."

"I've heard a lot about you, you're a beautiful girl."

She smiles awkwardly, says, "Thank you."

"Well can I get you anything? Something to drink, I don't have anything cooked so I can't offer you that."

"No ma'am, just a seat if that's okay."

"Yeah sure. I guess that would make sense considering you're about to pop and all. Go ahead and take a seat over there on the couch."

I watch her closely as she maneuvers around a stack of boxes and the coffee table to get to the couch, nervous that she might trip and fall.

"It's only a few more boxes that need to be loaded up. I'll put them in your car and we can hit the road."

His voice is steady but his eyes tell me he is ready to get the hell out of dodge. I waste no time grabbing boxes two at a time and lugging them to the car. The process takes no more than fifteen minutes. Hell, I could have told Farah to wait in the car for all of this.

"Jaime, it's time to go."

Mrs. Peters is standing at the bottom of the steps with her hand pressed against her hip. His little feet echo loudly against the hardwood floors thumping soundly on the carpeted steps until he reaches the bottom. He is tall for his age with a bright, toothy smile. It's eerie how much he looks like me and I can only conclude that to the fact that Elliott and I *are* brothers.

"Slow down!" Elliott commands. "You need some brakes on those feet. Say hello to your uncle Grayson and Auntie Farah."

His big bold eyes look up at me, yanks on my heart's strings. "Hi," he says coyly.

He wraps his little arms around my leg in an attempt to hug me before rushing over to Farah.

"Is there a baby in there?"

She giggles. "Yes, there is a baby in there."

"Can I feel?"

Farah takes his tiny hand and places it on the side of her tummy. His eyes are big as quarters with excitement.

"It's moving!"

"She is moving...*it* is a she. She is active right now; she's probably a little hungry."

"Like my sister, you mean?"

She smiles, says coolly, "If you want her to be."

"Ok buddy, come on and put your coat on."

"But daddy, I was playing with my sister," he says with a pout.

"You can go over Auntie Farah's house tomorrow and play with her all you want but we have to get going."

I help my wife to her feet, bid our farewells to Mrs. Peters before heading out to the car.

"It was good seeing you again Grayson, you haven't changed."

"Nice seeing you again as well. Take care of yourself."

She forces a smile my way. It is one masked with sadness though she is trying hard to hide it.

"You too."

As we leave Delaware, an intricate chapter in my life is closing while another is opening up for my brother. It is especially difficult considering the circumstances. I know that every time I look at my nephew, I will constantly be reminded of the woman I once loved. I am finally able to say that I am okay with that. It took me a long time to realize that I was allowing this situation to hinder me in ways I had yet recognized. I can finally put my hurt and pride behind me in order to be there for the people that love and need me most, my family.

| Welcome Home

My eyes fight against the overbearing brightness of the ceiling lights. The beeping of the heart monitor echoes inside of my head. My mouth feels like cotton, my temples throb. The IV in my arm is restricting me from making much movement. When I can finally put everything into focus, I see Grayson sitting beside me with his head rested on the bed. I stir as much as I possibly can to wake him; my arm feels like a ton of bricks. I am tired, so tired and sore. I wonder how long I have been sleep. Whatever drugs the doctor gave me put my ass out. Vigilantly, I manage to struggle my way into a sitting position. I see the bassinette next to Grayson and I can't help my smile. She is here.

It is Wednesday night, technically early Thursday morning. All I can feel is pain, so much it jars me from my sleep. I have been encountering some pain on and off for the last two months but the doctor says it is normal considering how close to my due date I am. Early contractions she calls them. I think nothing about it but the pulling feeling on my bladder forces me out of bed. Jaime is on me like a leech, his leg thrown over my thigh and arm rested on my belly. Elliott is in Atlanta on business and won't be back until the weekend. For the past two nights, I have awakened to this little boy draped over me like a sheet. He goes to bed one way and wakes up every which a way but straight. I peel him off of me slowly climbing out of bed. It is any day now for Nia. The weight of being pregnant is now uncomfortable and I can't express how anxious I am for this to all be over. I let the light from the television illuminate my path to the bathroom, careful not to trip on the toy truck in the middle of the floor. Sleeping through the night is almost impossible at this point. I rouse every night around the same time like clockwork but this time it's two hours before my usual wake up moment. Before I can make it to the toilet, before the light switch can even leave my finger good, a wave runs through me spilling over into the floor. For a minute, I think I have waited too long to get up to use the bathroom. I am embarrassed though there is no one awake to witness my carelessness. Hurriedly, or at least as fast as my swollen feet will take me, I go to grab a few dirty towels to clean my mess. A crippling pain ignites through my body, up through my back as if someone has just kicked me from behind. I double over resting my hands on my knees, gripping them roughly in a failed attempt to channel the pain elsewhere. It hurts so badly, my eyes water. I have never been good with pain, not physical pain, mental pain, and emotional pain, none of it. Even though I have tattoos, that hurting is nothing compared to what I am feeling now. The twinge subsides and I can finally stand up straight again. I abandon my mess rushing back into the bedroom, my panties soaked against me.

"Grayson," I try my best to whisper into the darkness loud enough for him to hear and for Jaime not to wake.

He is deep in sleep, snoring. Once I am close enough, I shake him violently not giving a fuck about his slumber. His eyes fly open in my direction. I am unable to speak as another spurt of pain tears through me, my fingers gripping the sheets.

"Baby...Farah, what's wrong?"

I am in labor and it is the most delayed comprehension ever. With much desperation, I try to grasp onto what little composure I have left. All the while, Grayson is scrambling from beneath the sheeted prison his legs are tangled in. There is no discretion about it and in another second Jaime is awake too.

"Farah, are you in labor? Baby, talk to me."

After several attempts, I manage to push the word "yes" from my mouth. You would have thought I told him the house was on fire the way he runs around the room. He is fully dressed before I can even peel my panties off of me.

"Auntie, what's wrong?"

I pull my bottom lip in between my teeth at the feel of another contraction coming on. I am trying to keep it together; I don't want him frightened by any of this.

"Your sister is coming," I tell him with a forced smile.

"Come on buddy," Grayson stammers. "Let's get dressed and leave auntie alone. She's in a little bit of pain."

He leaps from the bed over to Grayson who is waiting with a pair of sweatpants and a sweatshirt to dress him in.

"Why is she in pain?" he quizzes obediently putting one foot at a time into the pants leg.

"Nia is trying to make her grand entrance; she's just a little impatient so it's causing her some pain."

"Oh," he says as though he has just had an epiphany.

It takes twenty excruciating minutes to put on enough clothes to be properly covered for the cool morning air. Grayson calls my parents and sister while I dress. Jaime is running around excitedly downstairs hollering about his sister being on her way.

The sky is still dark as the morning hours creep in. With one hand on my belly and the other on the wheel, Grayson speeds down the highway in the direction of the hospital.

"I'm in labor, not being chased," I retort. "Please slow down with Jaime in this car."

"I'm sorry, I'm really fucking nervous."

"Language!" I holler.

"Okay! I'm sorry. Shoot, this is nerve racking."

"I know baby. I need you....I need you to be focused and *slow down!*"

By the time we reach the entrance to the emergency room, my contractions are at most two minutes apart. The car is still running and as scatterbrained as Grayson is right now, I am happy he remembered to put it in park before dashing inside for assistance.

"I'll hold your hand while Uncle Grayson is gone," Jaime pipes wrestling out of his car seat.

I clench my eyes shut, take a deep breath, say, "Oh sweetheart, it's okay. I don't want to hurt you; this pain is a little intense."

He frowns at me. "What is intense?"

I use the breathing techniques I learned in Lamaze class to get me through another contraction before replying, "Intense is when something is really, really strong."

"It's okay because I am an intense boy. You won't hurt me."

I let out a painful chuckle as he pushes his tiny hand into mine. I hold it lightly all while gripping the door handle for dear life.

It takes Grayson five of the longest, most painful minutes of my existence to return with two nurses in tow. One of them, a tanned woman with dark green eyes, is pushing a wheelchair. It feels like a scene from a movie rushing through the hallways of the hospital to the delivery room. Everything is happening so fast, I can barely focus. All I can feel is pain and too much of it.

"She's contracting fast," one of the nurses yells out.

I don't know which one. My eyes are clenched shut fighting against the pain thumping through me.

I am in and out. I feel weak with each contraction. How the hell am I suppose to deliver a baby when I can barely hold my head up. Hurriedly, they transfer me to a bed tearing at my clothes until they are off.

"Oh sis, I'm here." Clarissa's voice reverberates against my skull. "Nurse she looks so pale, why does she look like that?"

Machines whir around me, I feel the IV penetrating my arm. I hear Dr. Simmons but I can't see her, I can barely open my eyes. "We're going to have to do an emergency cesarean. Her blood pressure is dropping."

"What does that mean?" Grayson's tone is sharp mixed with fear.

"Relax Mr. Powell; we are going to take great care of her. We have to move her into surgery so we can deliver this baby."

My eyes flutter open and Grayson is standing over me, speaking inaudibly. There is an oxygen mask over my face. My vision is slightly blurred. When they open again, he is still there smiling down at me as he cradles our daughter in his arms. And then everything around me fades to black.

I reach out and run my free hand over his hair, down over his neck where I trail my fingernails to and fro. He moves groaning loudly as he lifts his head to look at me.

Smiling groggily, he says, "Hey mommy."

His smile is contagious forming mine at the corners of my mouth.

"Hey daddy."

He pushes to his feet planting a kiss on my forehead. "You scared me Farah. I thought for a moment I might lose you."

"Don't say that, I'm here. How long have I been sleep?"

"You've been out since yesterday morning. Nia was born at 6:20AM, it's after midnight."

"Can I have some water?"

The more I talk, the harder it becomes to swallow. He pours water from the pitcher sitting on the metal bed table into a Styrofoam cup, sticks a straw inside, and brings it to my lips. The liquid is warm yet still soothing to my parched throat.

I drink every drip drop in the cup, quenched. "Where is everybody?"

"Well baby, it's late. Your parents and sister will be back in a few hours and I'll call Elliott later on and tell him you are awake so he and Jaime can visit."

"How is she?"

He smiles and I can tell he is so in love. "She's looks just like you. She is amazing."

"I'm sorry for worrying you. I don't know what happened."

He sighs heavily. "I don't either but it scared the hell out of me. For a minute, I thought about what would happen if I lost you. I lost myself. It was a lot to bear."

There is so much emotion in his voice, so much need and it makes my heart ache.

Noticing the tears pillowing in my eyes, he says quickly, "But they said you just needed your rest and you would be okay. You probably want to hold your daughter now, huh?"

"Yes please."

Gently, carefully as if she is a fragile parcel, he scoops her up into his arms. He settles her into the crook of my own. Her skin is smooth. She is tiny and they have her wrapped up like a little baby burrito. I inhale her sweet scent, plant kisses on her cheeks. I want to see her eyes but she is so deep into sleep like she just worked two jobs and had to drive hours to get home. Nonetheless, I am instantly in love with this replica of me. She is not just amazing but beyond the perfection I conjured up in my dreams. Tears fall helplessly, I am overwhelmed. Grayson settles himself on the edge of the bed wrapping his arm around us. My family is complete: I have a wonderful and loving husband and a beautiful baby girl. Everything I have ever truly wanted, I have received. Every rollercoaster ride, every tear I have shed has all been worth it for this moment right here. Who could ask for more than this? Certainly, not me. That would just be too selfish. So I will just take all that I have and cherish it...one soul at a time.

Dear Love,
I am so happy to have met you.
Forever & Always,

- Farah Powell

| Epilogue

The house has finally settled for the night. Dinner has been served, the kids have eaten. Nia is sleeping soundly in her bed and Jaime has gone home for the evening. The only thing missing is my husband. It's exactly eight o' clock and I know that for the reason that I have been checking the time frequently in anticipation of his arrival home from a business dinner that has run over time.

"I should be home no later than seven, seven-thirty," he says at the eighth hour of the morning before he leaves to go into the office.

Now here it is a whole hour later and I have rearranged the rose pedals on the bed about ten times. It's our five year anniversary. Five whole years of marital harmony and every day feels like the first day I met him. It's a Tuesday and I have to wait two whole days before we can truly celebrate alone amongst lavish dining, passionate lovemaking in a hotel room, and spa style pampering. I get so anxious just thinking about it. I hear the door open and close downstairs. I shuffle into the bathroom to check my appearance. It hasn't changed since I looked five minutes ago but I find something to adjust. I fix my breasts in the black lace Victoria Secret push-up bra. They have swelled an entire cup size but I must say they look perched tonight. The black lace thong to match is slightly uncomfortable but I withstand it only for this special occasion. I close the silk robe over my protruding stomach. I am closing in on my eighth month of pregnancy, a little baby Grayson we have decided to name him. He has been kind to my body unlike Nia. My feet haven't swelled and my nose hasn't spread one bit. His footsteps thump against the carpeted stairs and I rush to be present when he enters the room. The first two buttons of his dress shirt are undone. His tie hangs lazily around his neck. His suit jacket is thrown across his arm. He looks so five o'clock right now. A twinge of a smile hits his lips as his eyes settle on what is before him. The room is littered with sweet smelling vanilla candles. Dozens of rose pedals are strewn over the bed. Atop those is a box of chocolate covered strawberries. A bottle of expensive red wine sits on the dresser with two chilled glasses in the offing to be poured into. A large box wrapped in shiny red wrapping paper sits in the middle, there's a black envelope on top that requires his opening.

"Happy Anniversary, Mr. Powell."

His eyes run the length of my frame. He licks his lips deliciously moving over to where I am standing.

"Mrs. Powell, you didn't have to do all of this."

He is so close, his cologne drawing me in. I can feel his erection growing against my thigh, his breath warm against my lips as he bends to kiss me. It is sensual, raw with passion. Ten fingers in my hair, he grips gently deepening the kiss. His tongue invades my mouth and it takes everything in me to keep my knees from buckling under his touch. My fingers work meticulously at his belt buckle pulling his dress shirt from the waistband to gain full access to all of the buttons. One by one I undo them, my eyes fixed on his.

"This is exactly what I need after the day I had," he breathes.

"It's just something to show you how much I love you after five years of marriage."

He smirks. "You show me that every day. Happy Anniversary, I love it."

I am aching to have him inside of me and judging by the bulge in his pants, his erection can't hold out much longer either.

"I'm glad to hear that."

He steps back to look at me, fingers the hem of my robe. "What's underneath?"

I grin deviously. "You should open your real gift before you undo me."

He chuckles, "You're right."

He reaches for the envelope first running a single finger under the flap to open it. He pulls out the itinerary for our getaway weekend, spa passes and restaurant reservations.

"My wife is so sneaky," he says with a laugh. "How did I miss this on the credit card statement?"

I giggle. "I didn't use it. You may be my husband and all but momma's got her own money too."

He shakes his head with a smile. "Now I know how you got all those shoes in the closet and in my daughter's closet. Duly noted, Farah Elise."

Next he tears at the wrapping paper on the box, eagerly pulling the top off. Inside are two separate boxes: one casing a Michael Kors watch he has had his eye on for the last month and the other a diamond studded wedding band to replace the one on his finger. I do the honors of putting on his new ring. It is a perfect fit.

"You never cease to amaze me, I swear. Thank you so much."

He kisses me fully, thankfully.

"I have to get your gifts from downstairs."

I take the box from his hands setting them on the floor. I move the box of chocolate covered strawberries and as gracefully as I can manage without looking like a whale on dry land, I settle myself in the middle of the bed.

"You have one more gift to open, Mr. Powell."

Ever so slowly he unravels me flying south on his private jet of ecstasy. He takes me higher and higher. And as I fall, I fall in love with this man named Grayson Powell like it's the very first time.

A First Look:

What Happened on Jaybird Street

I Winter

Winter 1999

"You got enough heat back there girl?"

The light blue Honda Civic reeks of cigarette smoke. Beneath me is tattered cloth seats that once were a rich beige color turned brown from years of wear and tear. It rattles obnoxiously when started up and the screeching noise when it stops is ear splitting. Nonetheless, my aunt is determined to get us from New York to Virginia in this thing. It has been three hours and she has been playing Destiny's Child *The Writing's on the Wall* album nonstop. If I didn't know what a bug-a-boo was before, I damn sure know what it is now.

"Yes ma'am," I mutter.

I pull my *North face* jacket tighter around my frame; bury my hands inside of the pockets. I am lying like a rug. There isn't enough heat pumping in this car to warm up a mouse. I refrain from telling her this though. If I have to hear about how my Uncle Theodore called himself getting the heat fixed by some crack head up in Brooklyn for fifty dollars again, I'm going to scream. If it was up to me, I would have kept my black ass in New York. It wasn't up to me though. After my mom passed last month, Aunt Brenda and Uncle Theodore have been trying to push me off on my grandmother. I can't blame them. Jointly, they can barely rub two quarters together to keep their car running let alone take in another child. Belinda Robinson—Linda is what everyone called her—died from breast cancer. My mom was here one day and gone the next. She raised me all by her lonesome in a studio apartment up in Queens. My father wasn't shit and left her high and dry before I could even make it into this world. It was just she and I until she met Tyrone Kinsley that lived off of Linden Boulevard. He was a cool dude, real flashy. He could be so corny sometimes with that fake ass five dollar gold tooth he always wore. He drove buses for a living. Corny or not, he made mad money and gave the best birthday and Christmas gifts too. He bought me a portable CD player for Christmas and I would be listening to it right now had the batteries not died on me. He really stuck with my mom while she battled that cancer. He would come and stay with me when she was in the hospital some nights and he even shoveled out dough to keep the lights on when all of hers was going toward hospital bills. Good ole Tyrone turned out to be good for nothing Tyrone. Before the dirt could even settle on her grave, he disappeared from the face of the earth. Come to find out, he had a whole wife *and* two kids outside of my mother. Niggas, I tell you. I always wondered why he never moved in even after being with my moms for ten years. I got the answer to that question.

I miss her. I miss her smell, her voice. Hell, I even miss the ass beatings she used to give me whenever I would get caught playing in her makeup. You only get one mother and now mine is dead and gone. I try not to think about it too much even though it is all still fresh. I don't know when I will ever see Queens again. The friends I made over my thirteen years of existence will now become memories of the past.

My whole life is about to change and there is nothing I can do about it.

COMING SUMMER 2015

CPSIA information can be obtained at www.ICGtesting.com
Printed in the USA
LVOW12s1430190215

427558LV00007B/895/P

ML   7-15